Where's the Baby?

by PAT HUTCHINS

A Mulberry Paperback Book • New York

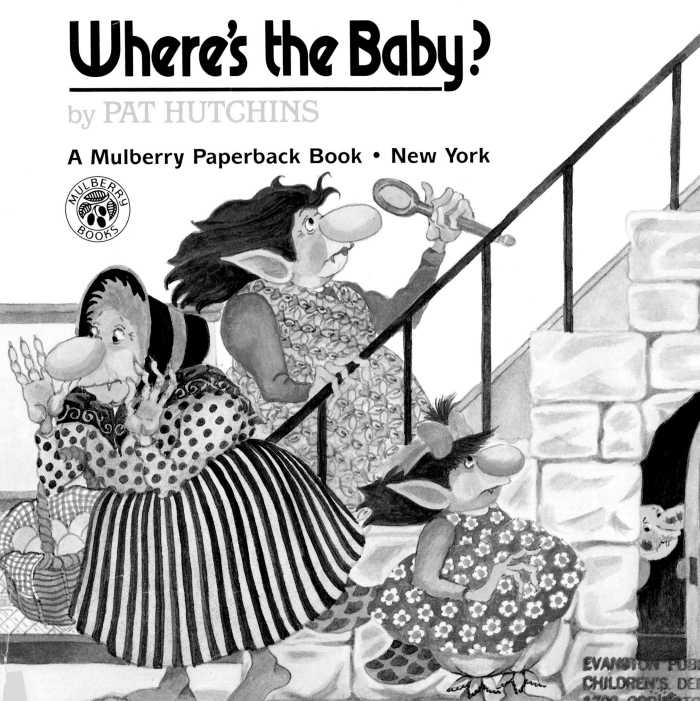

The Library of Congress has cataloged the Greenwillow Books edition
of *Where's the Baby?* as follows:
Hutchins, Pat (date)   Where's the baby?
Summary: When Grandma, Ma, and Hazel Monster want to find Baby Monster,
they follow the messy trail he has left.
ISBN 0-688-05933-3 (trade)
ISBN 0-688-05934-1 (lib. bdg.)
[1. Monsters—Fiction. 2. Babies—Fiction. 3. Cleanliness—Fiction.] I. Title.
PZ7.H96165Wh 1988 [E] 86-33566

1 3 5 7 9 10 8 6 4 2
First Mulberry Edition, 1999
ISBN 0-688-17063-3

FOR OUR KELLY

"Where's the baby?" Grandma cried.

"In the garden," Ma replied.

"Making a mess," said Hazel.

"Oh dear!" Ma shouted in alarm
grabbing hold of Grandma's arm,
"he's gone!"

But Hazel noticed on the floor
footprints in the corridor.
"They lead to the kitchen,"
Hazel cried,

and everybody rushed inside.

The mixture for the chocolate cake,
that Ma was just about to bake,
was tipped on the table and spilled on the floor
and made sticky fingerprints on the door.
"He's a help in the kitchen," said Grandma.

They followed the fingerprints on the wall
towards Pa's workroom in the hall.

Hazel opened the door and they all peered in.

"How clever!" said Grandma. "He's opened a tin!"

Paint trickled and dripped all over Pa's tools,

and lay on the floor in glossy pools.

"He's taken a brush," said Hazel.

The wall from the workroom was striped in red.

"It stops at the living room," Hazel said.

"He's good at painting," said Grandma.

"What a help!" Grandma said. "What a lot he can do,
he's been cleaning the living room chimney for you!"
The new white carpet was not so white,
and fingerprints as black as night
covered the sofa and both the chairs,
circled the walls—

then went upstairs.

"He's a good little climber," said Grandma.

They followed Hazel
who raced ahead,

into the bathroom the fingerprints led.

"How smart!" Grandma cried.

"To turn on the cold faucet

he must know blue is cold,

and the red one is hot!"

Talcum powder was thick on the floor,

and little white footprints went out of the door.

Ma and Pa's bedroom door was ajar.

"I'm sure I closed it this morning," said Ma.

"He must have opened it on his own,
I keep forgetting how much he's grown!"

"He's tall for his age," said Grandma.

The dress Ma was making was shorter than planned.
"He can use scissors," said Grandma. "Isn't that grand!"
The scarf Ma was knitting for Uncle Fred
had been unraveled all over the bed.
Wool wiggled and curved across the floor,
and they followed the wiggles out of the door.

"Oh dear," said Ma, "where can he be?"
"Don't worry," said Grandma cheerfully.
"I'm sure that we will find him soon,
 he's probably tidying Hazel's room."

All Hazel's books had been pulled from the shelf.
"He must have been trying to read them himself,"
said Grandma, "and look how he tried to write on the wall.
It's hard to believe he's a baby at all!"

There was one room left. . . .

So they tiptoed in. A tiny room as neat as a pin.

Not a toy out of place or a mark on the wall.

"He can't have been in here at all,"

said Ma. "It's far too clean."

But she hadn't seen what Hazel had seen.

"Oh!" cried Grandma, "isn't he sweet!"

"Yes," said Hazel, "when he's asleep."

"He does sleep soundly," said Grandma.

Legend
of
the
Lake

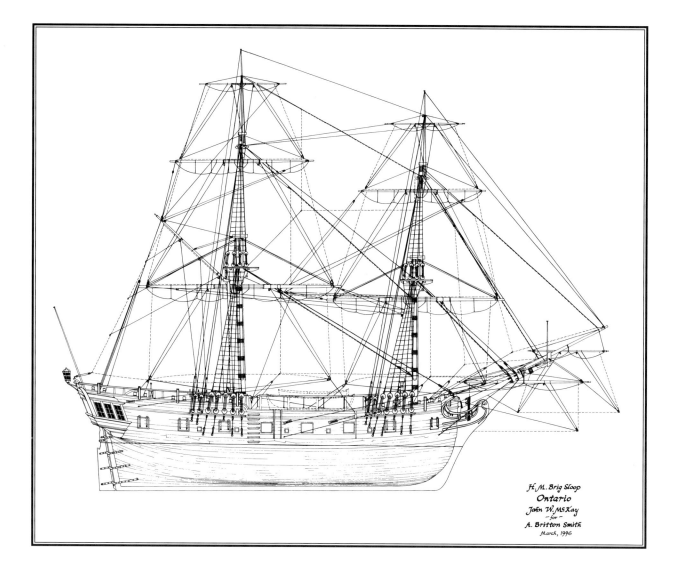

H. M. Brig Sloop
Ontario
John W. McKay
- for -
A. Britton Smith
March, 1996

Legend
of
the
Lake

THE 22-GUN BRIG-SLOOP

ONTARIO

1780

ARTHUR BRITTON SMITH
MC, CD, Q.C., LL.D., LL.B., B.SC. (Mil.)

with ship drawings by

JOHN W. MCKAY

Quarry Press

Text copyright © A. B. Smith, 1997.

Drawings copyright © John McKay, 1996-97.

Canadian Cataloguing in Publication Data

Smith, A Britton
    The legend of the lake : the Ontario, 1779-80

Includes bibliographical references.
ISBN 1-55082-186-5

    1. Ontario (Ship). 2. Ontario--Social life and customs. I. Title.

VA400.5.05S65 1996 359.3'22 C96-900981-X

Design by Susan Hannah.

Printed and bound in Canada by Friesens, Altona, Manitoba.

Published by Quarry Press, Inc.,
P.O. Box 1061, Kingston, Ontario K7L 4Y5.

Large scale reproductions of John W. McKay's drawings of *Ontario* are available by writing to the publisher.

All royalties from the sale of *Legend of the Lake* will be donated to the Marine Museum of the Great Lakes, Kingston, Ontario.

Acknowledgements

The author is indebted to many people who have assisted in the preparation of this account, and to The Marine Museum of the Great Lakes at Kingston, The National Archives of Canada, Queen's University Archives, The Metropolitan Toronto Reference Library, The Hector Foundation, Old Fort Henry, The Maclachlan Woodworking Museum, Cataraqui Archeological Foundation, The National Maritime Museum (U.K.), The Royal Ontario Museum, The Canadian War Museum, The St Lawrence River Historical Foundation, and The Kingston Public Library.

Noah Webster defined "Legend", as "A non-historical narrative," which this account, generally speaking, is. However a little history does creep in, here and there, because the source material is largely archival. People were pretty good about saving old letters, reports and orders back in the eighteenth century. Additional descriptive detail is occasionally borrowed from other settings; particularly the timber dimensions, which are based on what is left of several period brigs built on the lakes.

Correspondence dealing with the Provincial Marine or simply "Naval Department" during the Revolutionary War, usually refers to the King's vessels by name alone. Use of the words "His Majesty's Ship" is rare. The exception is found in printed receipts for cargo. These were signed by merchants to clear the captains upon delivery: for example;

"His Majesty's Arm'd Snow Rebecca,
Commander Lieutenant James Graham"
and
"His Majesty's Ship Limnade, Commander D.Betton, Esq "

so the term was official and regular use for vessels of the Provincial Marine. The abbreviation "H.M.S" was not employed until about 1800, so perhaps is not appropriate for *Ontario*.

A humble apology is tendered to John McKay for straying in the text, occasionally, from the detail of his fine drawings. Mr. McKay is internationally recognized as an authority in his field, and is the author and illustrator of books about HMS *Victory* and *Bounty*, among others. The drawings are based upon Royal Navy conventions of the day, for ships built in England and as seen on the Admiralty Draught. The text is in keeping with ship building techniques employed on the lakes, which allowed for severe ice conditions.

CONTENTS

Ontario *off* Fort Niagara.

Foreword

O N CHRISTMAS EVE 1678 Robert Cavelier, Sieur de la Salle, sailed out of Cataraqui harbour in his little *Frontenac*, a 25 ton barque built that year. His destination was Niagara and his cargo the materials with which to build *Griffon* on Lake Erie. Winter navigation on Lake Ontario is fate-tempting and, predictably, *Frontenac* was driven ashore. She broke up on January 8, 1679, a few leagues east of the Niagara River. No lives were lost, but very little cargo was salvaged.

A century after this first disaster and, at almost the same location, came the worst shipwreck in the lake's history. A short sail to the west of *Frontenac's* remains, under the silt and debris on the bottom, lies one of the lake's greatest treasures, *Ontario*, a long-forgotten Canadian sloop-of-war, built at the Carleton Island Shipyard in 1779-80. The largest vessel on the Great Lakes up to that time, she measured 226 tons burthen, and stretched 80 feet on the lower deck. Overall, including bowsprit, her length totalled 123 feet. The commodore's swallow-tailed pendant flying from her top-gallant mast was just 100 feet above the keel.

Ontario foundered during the night of October 31/November 1, 1780 in a sudden violent storm or hurricane, which struck out of the north-east at about 8:00 p.m. In her wreckage, and nearby, lie the bones of at least eighty-eight men, women, and children. There were no survivors. Of all of her passengers and crew, only six bodies were ever found. These came to the surface the following

Major General Jeffery Amherst (1717 - 1797) was later promoted to Field Marshal and given a peerage in recognition of his part in the winning of Canada.

July and are buried near Wilson, New York, a village about twelve miles east of Niagara, but the location of these graves is long lost.

The correspondence in the well-known Haldimand Papers and other collections of eighteenth-century letters held by National Archives of Canada gives minimal information about this ship. No story was published at the time, probably to delay leakage to General Washington of a valuable piece of intelligence. The military role of the armed vessels on Lake Ontario was to prevent an American attack on Montreal via the Mohawk and St. Lawrence Rivers. The feasibility of this route had been proven in 1760 by British Major-General Jeffrey Amherst, who, with a force of eleven thousand men and three hundred boats, descended on Montreal to capture the city and end the domain of France in Canada.

The loss of this new brig, mounting 22 guns, seriously reduced the deterrent value of the British squadron, especially since the next largest vessel, *Haldimand*, was in poor repair and out of action. So the secret was kept. To this day, many of the books on lake shipwrecks are wildly inaccurate in their accounts of *Ontario*. To muddy the water further, an earlier *Ontario* was badly damaged at Oswego by General Montcalm in 1756, and another ship of the same name scuttled or wrecked off the same port a few years later. This *Ontario* II was probably the frame of a schooner captured by Amherst at the French shipyard on Point au Baril, near present-day Maitland, in August 1760, and subsequently completed by the British. She may have been a sister ship of *Iroquoise* and *Outouaise*, the last two corvettes launched by the French before the surrender. If so, she was about one hundred and fifty tons.

The late C. H. J. Snider, a foremost authority on early sail on Lake Ontario, believed that Montcalm repaired *Ontario* I to transport captured stores and guns back to Cataraqui. The French did not change her name, as they did with two other captured ships, and she was one of the vessels taken and burned at Fort Frontenac in 1758. He was sure that the prow of a ship dug up in 1953 during the

The British squadron on Lake Ontario in 1756.
Ontario I *is the small sloop on the right.*
From a painting by C.H.J. Snider.

Prow of Ontario I? The identity of this artifact, now on display at the Marine Museum of the Great Lakes in Kingston, Ontario, is still uncertain.

excavation for Normandy Hall, at the Army Staff College, Kingston, belonged to her. Evidence of repaired shot damage convinced him, because the French-built vessels had never suffered gunfire, although the British-built had. If indeed it is she, the rest of *Ontario* I still lies under the lawns beside Ontario Street. She was 45 feet in length, 15 in beam, 7 in depth and 60 tons, carrying five 4-pounder guns and one 3-pounder.

Why is the third vessel of the name such a treasure? To begin with, when she sank she was new, fully armed and equipped. She did not break up, except for the loss of part of one quarter-gallery, and this was probably smashed by a fallen mast. She lies in cold, dark, deep water where decay is slow. She is partially buried in silt and is beyond the reach of weekend divers and looters. The diver who identified the wreck, Mr. Richard Acer, reports that her hatches and cabin doors are jammed shut, evidence that her contents have not been disturbed. The jamming may have been caused by slight wracking of the hull when it struck the bottom or from uneven support over the two centuries in the silt.

On board one may expect to find sixteen 6-pounder guns and six 4-pounders; a dozen 1/2-pounder swivel guns; gun locks, sixty-odd Brown Bess muskets and bayonets, lanterns, many pistols, plates, cutlasses, swords, pikes, hatchets, badges, buttons, belt-plates, china, pewter, bottles, cooking pots, spoons, and ladles. Possibly a spy-glass, sextant, gorget, pocket compass, table silver, and other personal items belonging to the officers. Pipes, razors, knives, and tools of all kinds may be found in the many wooden barrack boxes. Some textiles may have survived, in tightly packed seaman's chests. All the personal kit of the 34th Regiment marine detachment which she carried was lost, not only that of the men on board, but of a considerable number (perhaps eighty) others of the 34th who were ashore on an October raid against the American rebel settlements. A letter written by their commander to Governor Haldimand sought compensation for these men.

When the vessel is photographed and carefully examined, it may be found that she is still sound enough to raise. Much older wrecks have been brought to the surface and settled in drydocks. The trick is to keep them wet while preservatives penetrate the wood fibres; otherwise, they quickly decay once exposed to air. An ideal site for such a project would be the graving dock at the Marine Museum of the Great Lakes in Kingston, Ontario.

Mary Rose in Portsmouth, Hampshire, U.K., and *Vasa* in Stockholm, Sweden, have led the way in marine archeology. The scientific advances in stabilization and preservation techniques have now reached a level at which the risk of leaving the wreck to the increased acidity of lake water outweighs the hazards of retrieval. The wreck of *Iroquoise* in the St. Lawrence River had lasted from the 1760s to the 1970s with many planks in place. Now she is down to bare frames. All her planking has vanished under pressure of time, current, and decay in the past 25 years. What the zebra mussels will do to this and other wrecks is unknown.

Such a project would require a submersible drydock of a size large enough to contain *Ontario* but still be able to enter the dock at Kingston. Something about 100 feet by 40 feet, with buoyancy tanks to lift her, is needed for the final journey to a secure berth. Interesting is the close proximity of the Marine Museum to *Ontario's* birthplace at Carleton Island, just 15 kilometres to the south-east.

Because only the port side of the upper deck is visible above the silt, the description and drawings offered here are based on the contemporary draught supplied from admiralty records, courtesy of the National Maritime Museum, Greenwich, U.K. Beyond that everything is conjecture. If and when a full examination is conducted, proper corrections and apologies will be made. Meanwhile the available information has been used to create a plausible account of *Ontario*, her construction, her crew, and her foundering in 1780. The story of *Ontario* begins, though, on New Year's Eve 1775, early in the American War of Independence as the British struggled to hold Canada against the Revolutionary Army of George Washington.

Ronald L. Way of Fort Henry (right) and C.H.J. Snider of "Schooner Days" (left) watch as the prow of what may be Ontario I *is raised in 1953.*

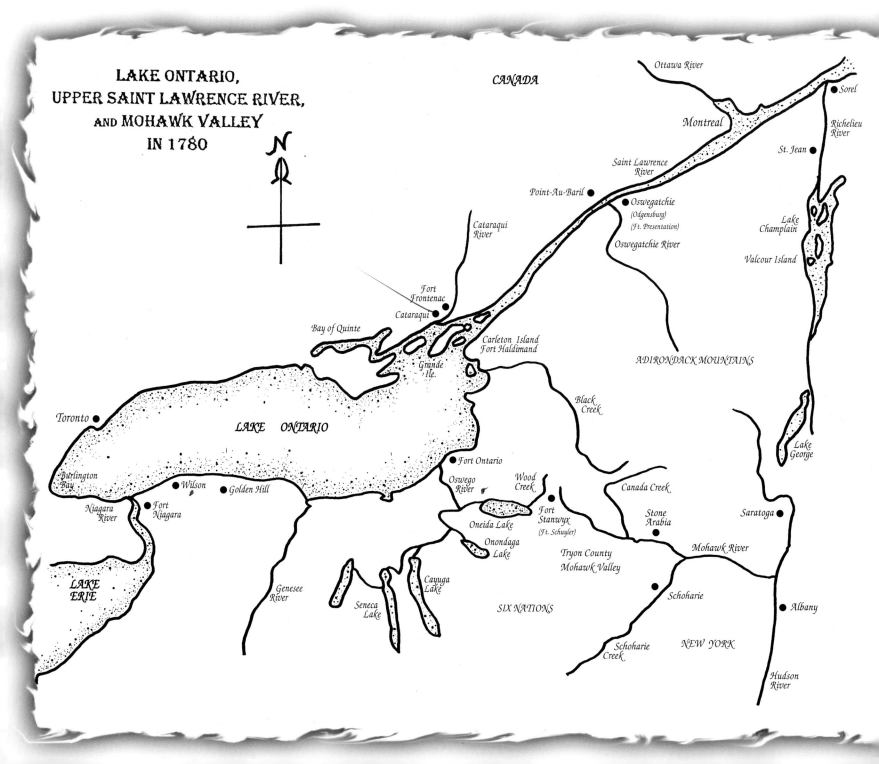

LAKE ONTARIO,
UPPER SAINT LAWRENCE RIVER,
AND MOHAWK VALLEY
IN 1780

N

CANADA

Ottawa River

Sorel

Montreal

Richelieu River

St. Jean

Saint Lawrence River

Point-Au-Baril

Oswegatchie
(Odgensburg)
(Ft. Presentation)

Lake Champlain

Cataraqui River

Oswegatchie River

Valcour Island

Fort Frontenac

Cataraqui

Carleton Island
Fort Haldimand

ADIRONDACK MOUNTAINS

Bay of Quinte

Grande Ile.

Black Creek

Toronto

LAKE ONTARIO

Lake George

Burlington Bay

Fort Ontario

Wood Creek

Canada Creek

Saratoga

Wilson

Golden Hill

Oswego River

Stone Arabia

Niagara River

Fort Niagara

Oneida Lake

Fort Stanwyx
(Ft. Schuyler)

Mohawk River

Onondaga Lake

Tryon County
Mohawk Valley

Schoharie

LAKE ERIE

Genesee River

Cayuga Lake

Albany

Seneca Lake

SIX NATIONS

NEW YORK

Schoharie Creek

Hudson River

Turning Point
for Canada

ON NEW YEAR'S EVE 1775, with food and fuel almost gone, besieged Quebec City was nearing surrender to the American invaders. The tide of battle turned when a surprise night attack by the Revolutionary Army, under cover of a heavy snowstorm, found the defenders sober and alert. Several hundred of the garrison were crew of His Majesty's *Frigate Lizard* and *Sloop Hunter,* men used to standing watch in bad weather. With no celebrations in progress, perhaps there was no liquor left in town! Somehow the powder was dry and the British gunners and Canadian militiamen were at their posts. Many Continental troops died in the snow that night. Four hundred and thirty-one more, who had fought their way determinedly to positions inside the walls, surrendered in the morning.

With their general killed in the streets of Lower Town, the remainder of the Americans lost the will to storm the walls again. They hung on until spring, and then retreated toward Montreal. Their troubles were far from over, however. Smallpox, against which the British and Canadian forces had been inoculated by deliberate infection with cowpox, a mild disease of dairy cattle, struck the Revolutionary troops with devastating results. Although a Quebec City physician, Dr. Buller, inoculated some captured Americans, the two hospitals of Montreal, The Hôtel Dieu and Les Fréres

Charron (run by The Grey Nuns), were packed with sick and dying soldiers. Strangely, many were clad in scarlet tunics. When their own supply routes were cut off by Canadian patrols, the Americans had been fortunate enough to capture a British store ship in the St. Lawrence. She was laden with infantry uniforms, tricorn hats, boots, gunpowder, and food intended for the defending British units. Another lucky find for the invaders was the foundry at St. Maurice, near Trois Rivieres. Here they were able to procure a supply of shot and shell for their artillery, made to order from Canadian iron.

With spring came also the realization that very few Canadians were sympathetic to the Revolution, and the survivors of the American army quietly withdrew up the Richelieu River whence they had come, not to abandon the cause, at all, but to gain strength for a new attempt. Every fighter wants a re-match when he does not win, and the American strategic planners firmly believed that all of British North America would soon be within their grasp, having eluded them by a hair.

On the other side, the British knew that they had themselves, in the previous war against France, successfully attacked Canada from the west, using a left hook down the St. Lawrence River. Next time, General Washington, they believed, would weigh the chances of a repeat invasion from Lake Ontario. To forestall this possibility, it was clear that the two British regiments garrisoning the western posts must be augmented, the few fighting vessels on Lake Ontario be increased in numbers and size, and an aggressive policy of hit-and-run raiding be immediately implemented by the new Loyalist ranger battalions against northern New York.

A squadron of small warships had been hastily built on Lake Champlain in 1776 and, at the battle of Valcour Island, inflicted a defeat on the American vessels, making secure this invasion route for the time being, at least. Lieutenant John Schank of the Royal Navy had distinguished himself in this victory as commander of *Inflexible*, a brig of 16 guns. He was born in Fifeshire, Scotland in

1740, went to sea as a volunteer at seventeen, served four years as a seaman, was appointed midshipman and commissioned lieutenant in 1776 at Quebec. He had also shown great resourcefulness in knocking apart the Royal Navy sloop *Maria* on the St. Lawrence and re-assembling her on the Richelieu River for use on Lake Champlain. The component parts were dragged many miles overland to avoid the rapids.

This energetic and resourceful officer was chosen to oversee the construction of a new Lake Ontario dockyard to produce vessels of various sizes in short order. In January 1778, he snow-shoed from Montreal to Niagara to view the country for himself and to check the availability of white oak and pine suitable for shipbuilding. This very difficult feat gives the measure of the man. In August 1778, Schank and a large party arrived at Deer (Carleton) Island by bateaux, pitched their tents, and went to work building whaleboats.

*D*espite the Revolutionary War, fur-trade continued to be the mainstay of the Canadian economy, and the trade required canoes, vessels, and bateaux, to transport the furs. Thousands of "packs of peltries," as they were called, travelled to Montreal from the interior. The major part of this product came down the Great Lakes and their tributary rivers, crossing Lake Ontario by schooner to Carleton Island. Often the schooners went a further 70 miles downstream to Oswegatchie (now Ogdensburg), particularly at the height of the season when the bateau brigades were swamped by sheer volume.

From Carleton or Oswegatchie the bales were carried to Lachine by bateau, a trip of three or four days, running the rapids. Coming back against the current meant anything from ten to fourteen days, depending on the wind and the cargo. Heavy loads meant slower progress. The bateaux travelled in brigades of three or more for mutual assistance at difficult places. The usual crew was

Lieutenant John Schank, RN, (1740-1823) in later life (c. 1805). Two epaulets denote post captain rank.

five *engagés* (contract oarsmen) plus a *conducteur* in charge of the brigade. To drag each boat up a number of the most turbulent rapids required the combined efforts of at least a dozen men. Some walked the gunwales shoving on iron-shod setting poles, while others waded along the shallows with the tracking line over their shoulders. At a few of the worst stretches, retired *engagés* had taken up residence and rented out yokes of oxen to assist. At the Cascades, and several other rapids, most up-bound cargo had to be portaged by ox cart. Only an empty bateau could be floated close enough to shore to avoid the fierce current.

Many of the trips were under charter to the army, moving soldiers, supplies, and arms to the western garrisons and Carleton Island. With ten or twenty strong young passengers to take the tow-ropes the time of travel was shortened considerably.

The army also helped in another way. Lieutenant William Twiss of the Corps of Engineers figured that a canal to circumvent the Cascade Rapid could be built in one year. General Haldimand agreed, remembering that this rapid had drowned eighty-four men when he made the trip with Amherst in 1760. An engineer company, with the help of hired draft animals and local men, did the job. Horses and scrapers excavated the loose earth. Oxen and dump-carts (loaded by hand) hauled it away. For the sake of speed, the canal was dug just wide enough and just deep enough to accommodate a bateau. It had three short sections, the longest just 400 feet. Each lock was only 6 1/2 by 40 with a depth of 2 1/2 feet over the sills. Some limestone was encountered. This required the manual drilling of holes with star drill and hammer, then loading and shooting with cartridges of black blasting powder.

Also to save time, the two locks were made initially of squared timbers, dove-tailed and tennoned together. Each crib was filled with rock, and the seams caulked. Permanent masonry locks would be built later. Meanwhile the urgent demands of the war must be heeded. Opening the canal in the fall of 1779 meant that cannon, cordage, anchors, and other awkward loads would no longer require a portage at the Cascades. By 1783 it included the Cedars rapids and had increased to five stone locks.

The bateaux then built at Lachine were from 36 to 40 feet in length, 6 feet broad at the widest point, and drew about 20 inches when loaded with 4 or 5 tons of freight. George Heriot, a few years later, described a bateau as 40 feet by 6 feet, carrying 25 barrels or 9,000 pounds weight. The bottom was made of red or white oak to stand the constant scraping on rocks and frequent beaching. The sides were "white fir," which might mean balsam or spruce. Stem and stern were both pointed and swooped up a foot or so higher than the nearly vertical sides. The mast carried a lug sail about fifteen feet high.

Heading up-river, loads could run to forty or fifty barrels of salt beef, salt pork, flour, peas, rice, oatmeal, and other supplies for the crews of the vessels and the garrison troops. Singing was the solace of the weary crews. One man would sing a line, which was then repeated by all. They would always sing when passing another bateau or approaching a landing. At night the crew cooked their own food, often salt pork and peas boiled in a big brass kettle. In 1795 Isaac Weld said the boatmen subsisted on salt pork, biscuit, pease, and brandy. A large vessel of porridge made from the first three ingredients was placed in the bow each morning to be eaten at the stopping place. Cucumbers were eaten large and yellow. A favourite dish was cucumber chopped up, skins included, with sour cream. They smoked ropey black twist tobacco incessantly in their clay pipes, measuring distance by the number of pipes smoked en route. One pipe equalled about three-quarters of a mile.

The whaleboats are not as well documented as the bateaux. Contemporary drawings show Lake Ontario whaleboats with quite massive stems, rather bluff bows, and notched gunwales for three or four oars a side. Two masts are standard, with various types of sails. A steering oar is favoured over a rudder.

A bateau running the Lachine Rapids, 1843.
From a painting by Col. H.F. Ainslie.

Captain Knox says each carried eight oars, twelve paddles, two setting-poles, one scoop, and about fourteen men. The paddles would be used for a short high-speed dash under fire in an assault landing. Major Robert Rogers visited Cataraqui in 1760 with two hundred of his rangers in fifteen whaleboats. That means thirteen or fourteen men per boat. Perhaps eight oars each, allowing five or six men to rest at a time. Navy specifications of a "whaler" call for a length of 25 feet, beam of 5 1/2 feet or 6 feet, depth of 2 feet 2 inches, and distance between thwarts of 2 feet 10 inches. Stem is "raking," stern "sharp," and weight 8 hundredweight. This boat sounds like one to carry fourteen men.

In the fall of 1778 at Carleton Island enough boats were built in a few weeks to transport a raiding party of battalion strength, about four hundred men, probably about thirty boats. This had to be a quick-and-simple type of boat, resembling a smaller scale bateau perhaps, likely made of cedar or spruce for lightness and portage-ability. The indicated size for fourteen men is something with four thwarts, say 20 or 22 feet long by 5 to 6 feet in beam, pointed at both bow and stern. Three men would sit on each thwart, one in the bow and one in the stern at the steering oar. This bateau would be fairly deep-sided to manage rough water and to accommodate soldier's kit and other baggage below the thwarts. For repeated use, such craft would have steam-bent oak ribs; oak stem, keel, and gunwales; clinker-built (lap-straked) with white cedar planking, clinched copper fastenings, and a rudder. This would be a true whaler meeting Admiralty specifications and good for many years. However, a one-trip expedition would be adequately served by a dory-like boat, made of wide boards by semi-skilled carpenters.

As the shipyard developed so did the social world on Carleton Island, where shipwrights, soldiers, traders, loyalist refugees, and their families formed a community centred at Fort Haldimand.

Whaleboat. From a painting by William Allen Wall.

The Carleton Island Shipyard

CARLETON ISLAND IS ONE of the larger of the Thousand Islands, lying about one mile east of Lake Ontario in the South Channel of the St. Lawrence River. It was called Ile aux Chevreuils or Ile Chevreux on French maps, then Deer Island by English speaking cartographers, and, occasionally, Buck Island by merchants.

Prior to Lieutenant Schank's arrival it had been a transfer point between river bateaux and lake schooners. A couple of log warehouses and a bunk house served the merchants needs. Then in August 1778, the island started a brief new life as a boat yard, building whaleboats for use in raids up the Oswego River, across Lake Oneida, and down the Mohawk Valley. The men of Butler's Rangers and of Johnson's King's Royal Regiment of New York (KRRNY) had farmed that part of New York State in happier times. Driven from their homes, the Loyalist soldiers struck time and again at the back door of the Revolutionary Army, drawing off troops that would otherwise have been available to fight the British forces on the Atlantic coast.

Whaleboats were nothing new on Lake Ontario. In 1756, a French bateau force from Fort Frontenac under General Montcalm had captured British-held Oswego, taking twenty-five hundred prisoners. Britain retaliated two years later, sending Lieutenant-Colonel John Bradstreet with a brigade of three thousand men in two hundred whaleboats up the Mohawk River, Wood Creek, Lake Oneida, Oswego River route to take Fort Frontenac and burn the French corvette and schooner squadron, trapped in the inner harbour. The next year, 1759, they came again, this time under Brigadier-General John Prideaux, to besiege Fort Niagara. When Niagara fell, the French forces at Detroit and further west were left with no supply route. For the Fort Niagara siege, Prideaux established a base at Oswego commanded by Swiss professional soldier Lieutenant-Colonel Frederick Haldimand. To protect his communications, Haldimand set up a shipyard at the river mouth, and by 1760 had launched several sizable vessels. These managed to wrest control of Lake Ontario and the St. Lawrence River from the French.

General Jeffrey Amherst then came up the Mohawk. His eleven thousand men included two battalions of the famous Black Watch (The Royal Highland Regiment). Assembling at Oswego, they rowed down the St. Lawrence to capture first the French Fort *La Presentation*, near present-day Ogdensburg, and next, after losing eighty four men in the rapids, Montreal.

Eighteen years later, in a different war, Frederick Haldimand was appointed governor and commander-in-chief of Canada. He brought to the post a good knowledge of the inland routes acquired during his earlier command and his boat trip down the river with General Amherst. Haldimand issued orders in July of 1778 for the re-establishment of the former French shipyard at Cataraqui, out of use for twenty years. He suggested Deer Island (soon to be re-named Carleton) as an alternate site, and his subordinates, after looking over both locations, elected to set up shop on Deer.

Cataraqui might have become a British garrison post in the summer of 1778 instead of waiting until five years later, except for a few negative factors turned up by the reconnaissance made on August 14th and 15th. One of the party, Captain René LaForce of the brig *Seneca* knew the harbour well, as he had previously served in the French squadron on the lake. Indeed, Bradstreet had

Sir Frederick Haldimand (1718 - 1791), a bilingual Swiss in the British Army, was promoted to general in the Revolutionary War and appointed Governor of Canada in 1778.

La Marquise de Vaudreuil	La Hurault	La Louise	Ontario I
(Capt. LaForce)	*(Capt. LaBroquerie)*		*(or* Le Saint-Victor*)*

Some of the French vessels on Lake Ontario in 1758.
From a painting by C.H.J. Snider.

Private and Officer and button of the 47th Regiment of Foot, c. 1778, parade-ground dress.

captured his vessel, *Marquise de Vaudreuil*, right there in the mouth of the Great River Cataraqui. After sounding the old anchorage, they found it too shallow for *Seneca*. She drew 11 feet fully laden. Besides, half a dozen French hulks littered the area, scuttled and burned to the waterline by Bradstreet. Furthermore, Lieutenant John Glennie R.A., another of the group, said the old fort was vulnerable to artillery sited on the high ground nearby, now the Queen Street parking lot above the current armory, west of Montreal Street, Kingston.

The force under Lieutenant Schank ascended the St. Lawrence from Montreal in a large convoy of many bateaux. All the tools and hardware needed to establish a boat-building operation and eventually a full shipyard were transported to Deer Island. The work force and protective garrison consisted of twenty-seven boat carpenters, two and a half companies of the 47th Regiment of Foot under Captain Thomas Aubrey, a Royal Artillery detachment under Lieutenant Glennie, and some engineers under Lieutenant William Twiss, a Canadian officer in the Corps of Engineers.

The 47th Foot (Loyal North Lancashires), strangely a largely Irish regiment, had been part of General Burgoyne's army at Saratoga. The disastrous defeat and surrender of the British force in that battle left most of the battalion prisoners of war, but Aubrey and two companies had been stationed on Diamond Island and missed the action. A few other men of the 47th left out of battle for sickness or other reasons also avoided the capitulation.

Captain Aubrey was a difficult man who fought constantly with both Lieutenant Glennie and Lieutenant Twiss. When it came time to map and name the area of Fort Haldimand, the Carleton Island redoubt, Twiss and Glennie selected the name "Aubrey Head" for the somewhat penis-shaped point at the west end of the island enclosing "Schank Harbour." Aubrey subsequently court-martialled poor Glennie for this and other insults, but the conviction was overturned on appeal.

All liked the prospect of easy defence at Deer Island. It had a bluff about sixty feet high on the westerly end. Below the bluff were two sheltered coves and, in between, a flat area suitable for shipbuilding. A battery of guns on the heights would dominate the main channel of the St. Lawrence and also protect the dock area. Winter-bound vessels, locked in the ice, would not be vulnerable to burning by overland raiding parties on snowshoes.

About mid-August 1778, work commenced in earnest. Lieutenant Twiss laid out earthworks as a start on the construction of Fort Haldimand atop the bluff. Sheds for boat building sprang up on the shore. A storehouse, carpenter shop, blacksmith shop, and hospital were completed. Two hundred pine logs and ten thousand shingles were cut for barrack blocks. A barrack was one hundred and seventy-four feet long with several massive stone chimneys, each containing two fireplaces back-to-back. One hundred and sixty to one hundred and eighty men were accommodated per block. Cargoes of planks and boards were off-loaded from the vessels, product of the saw mills at Niagara and Oswegatchie (now Ogdensburg).A few yoke of oxen and teams of horses were bought or hired from the scattered farms of the district. These lay mostly to the north, closer to old Fort Frontenac. A scow ferry shuttled to 'Grande Isle, later to be renamed Wolfe Island after General Wolfe, carrying produce and livestock for the growing garrison. Oats and harness were also purchased locally.

More brigades of bateaux arrived from Montreal with supplies of all sorts. Those soldiers in the ranks of the 47th experienced with axe and adze were employed in erecting the log barracks for the winter and in clearing a field of fire to the east of the fort, inland from the coves. Two companies of the King's Royal Regiment of New York, men from the upper part of that state recruited by Sir John Johnson, arrived from Quebec. These troops were needed to assist in construction of the fort, as well as to carry out raids.

Captain Aubrey wrote to Governor Haldimand in November of 1778 that a French trader was settled at Catarachie and that two Indian traders who lived beyond Catarachie had a large quantity of rum. There was not one drop of rum on Carleton Island, however. On November 17th Captain Aubrey reported that he had planted twenty apple trees. General Haldimand was always urging

A *Soldier's Life:*
haircuts (upper) and laundry (lower).
From a Microcosm by William H. Pyne.

his local commanders to grow food, but this was really looking into the future! A farmer was hired to tend the livestock and an extra baker was added to make bread for the Indians, many of whom were entitled to army rations as scouts for the Indian Department. A century later J.H. Durham found five mounds of bricks on the island, perhaps the remains of bread ovens at the vanished bakery, but they might also have been the masonry bases of boilers and steam boxes used by the shipwrights.

A Madame Mayrant requested permission to trade at Cataraqui. This implies that she planned to sell to servicemen as a sutler; otherwise, no license was required. Soldiers visiting Cataraqui may have been employed scavenging used bricks at the ruins, cutting locust wood for the shipyard, or harvesting hay for the animal's winter feed. The bricks salvaged at Fort Frontenac would come from derelict bake ovens and numerous fireplaces. James Peachey's drawing of the ruins shows eight massive chimneys in the two-storey French barracks. Each would have back-to-back hearths on both floors. An application was also received from J.C. Portier, Cataraqui, for a license to operate boats on the north shore of Lake Ontario. This is a puzzler, unless he planned a fore-runner of the Wolfe Island ferry to provide service between Cataraqui and the island. There was a two mile portage to connect with the boat from Carleton.

Another trader in the district was M. DuMoulin, who went into the woods offering his wares to the somewhat nomadic Mississauga Indians at their camp-sites. His service meant fewer visits to the Carleton island stores to sell venison. Indian hunters had become an important source of fresh meat. The resulting shortage induced Dr. Gill to request priority for his hospital patients in the allocation of deer carcasses, perhaps to relieve scurvy. Every winter this disease crippled many of the garrison because of the dependence on dry rations.

A number of wives of officers and soldiers came up river from their Montreal area homes and built cabins to be near their husbands. These people

A view of the ruins at the fort at Cataraqui, June 1783. From a painting by James Peachey.

were issued seeds and encouraged to grow garden produce for the garrison. The Iroquois drawn to the island had already started growing corn, squash, beans, and peas for their own use. Ginseng, a medicinal root highly prized in China, grew wild in the area. The natives gathered this in quantity and sold it to the merchants for cash, thus acquiring some purchasing power.

Trader Robert Hamilton opened a general store on Carleton in 1779 to cater to the needs of the garrison and the growing number of civilians employed in and around the dockyard. He was careful not to antagonize Monsieur J.C. Portier, the part-time trader-farmer at Cataraqui hamlet. M. Portier had been buying from the firm of Forsyth & Dyce for years, and their schooner made regular calls at his landing. Hamilton was local agent for that firm as well as for the Niagara merchant Thomas Robinson. Other merchants in business at Carleton Island were Alexander Campbell, Robert Macaulay, and Hugh Mackay. Mary Mackay, wife of Hugh, was officially the garrison commissary. The commissary was a civilian

Robert Hamilton, Merchant.

officer of the Quartermaster General who handled matters of supply, bread, pay, movement, and purchases of all manner of non-military stores. Other civilians, often wives of soldiers, were licensed as sutlers. These people drew the rations for their units and prepared the soldiers' food. They also sold spruce beer, rum, brandy, and a wide variety of canteen necessities, such as toffee, brushes, pipes, tobacco, soap, and letter paper. Their establishment, whether tent or log cabin, was the off-duty social centre for the junior ranks.

The officers held a weekly dance in their mess, attended by the merchants and any loyalists awaiting passage to Montreal. Ice fishing, sleighing parties, curling, and snow-shoeing were other winter pastimes and relief from garrison blahs. The long hill from the fort to the harbour provided a great sled run. This was a boon to the Iroquois who made and sold quantities of toboggans, as well as many pairs of snowshoes. Other articles of local manufacture dealt for the native people by the merchants were baskets, moccasins, blocks of dark,

A trading post c. 1780. From a drawing by C.W. Jeffreys.

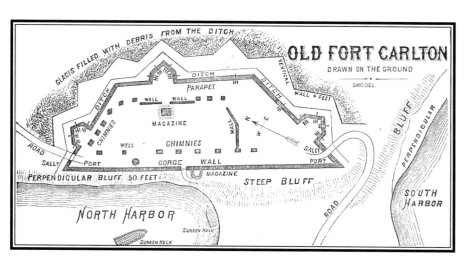

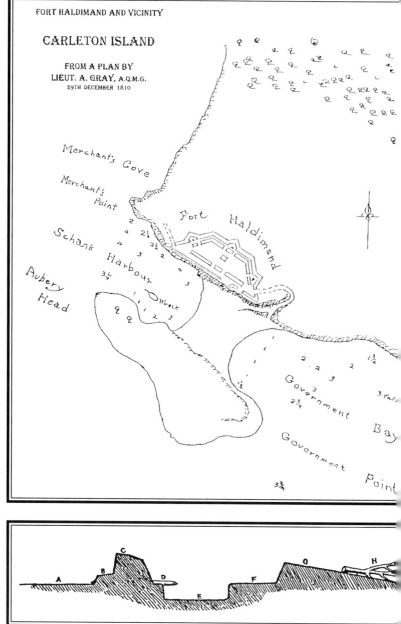

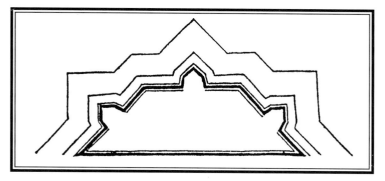

Upper Left: Plan of Fort Haldimand (a.k.a. Old Fort Carlton) from "A History of Jefferson County" published in 1878. The centre bastion is incorrectly located. Note the two hulks.

Lower Left: Plan of Fort Haldimand. Drawn in 1889 by J.H. Durham.

Lower Right: Cross section diagram and key below. By J.H. Durham.

Elevation — A, Terreplein; B, Banquet; C, Parapet; D, Fraise; E, Ditch; F, Covert-way; G, Glacis; H, Abatis

Upper Left: Barracks near Central Bastion in Fort Haldimand. Drawn in 1889 by J.H. Durham.

Lower Left: Barracks and powder magazine.

Upper Right: View of Fort Haldimand looking toward the North Salient.

Lower Right: Old chimney of the dockyard hospital.

Officer's uniform button of King's Royal Regiment of New York.

Mrs. Grant (née Marie Lemoyne, Baroness de Longeuil, called "Mimi Baronne") in later life.

hard, maple sugar, muskrat hats, clay preserve pots, ash paddles, and bark or dug-out canoes. Doeskin garments embroidered with porcupine quills and glass beads were popular items.

The Iroquois on Carleton Island were mostly Mohawks, friends of Molly Brant, consort of Sir William Johnson, and her brother, Captain Joseph Brant. Back home, they had been farmers, long converted to European methods of animal husbandry, agriculture, pottery, blacksmithing, and even masonry. Stone chimneys and mortared chinks in their long buildings were a great comfort. They still hunted and fished with the old skills, and found a ready market for surplus food at the fort commissary. Salmon, geese, ducks, venison, passenger pigeon, berries, mushrooms, clams, and wild rice graced the island tables in season. Everybody dined well.

In their off-duty hours soldiers of all ranks explored the river and countryside on duck shooting and deer hunting forays. Many of the Loyalist troops knew that no matter who won the war, they could never return to their pre-revolution homes and farms. To them the rich black humus of Grande Isle (Wolfe Island) appealed as a location for a post-war community. One of the more enthusiastic was Captain Donald Macdonald of the Royal Yorkers, KRRNY. He had been commissioned in North Carolina early in the war by King George III, a bit of a surprise considering that his mother, Flora Macdonald, was the self-same Flora who accompanied Bonnie Prince Charlie over the sea to Skye after the 1745 Highland Rising. Serving the king, real or pretender, was a family thing! In due course Captain Macdonald did indeed become a farmer on Wolfe Island and some of his descendants are there today. He himself died on the Island in 1839, aged 97. Other garrison members from Fort Haldimand were granted land in several nearby townships after the peace. These included men of the KRRNY, 8th, 34th, and 47th foot. The Mohawk scouts and their kinsmen were given Tyendinaga township at Deseronto, named after their leader, Captain Joseph Brant.

Captain David Alexander Grant, of the 84th, Royal Highland Emigrants, married Marie Lemoyne, 4th Baroness de Longeuil, in 1781. He was still stationed at Carleton Island in October 1783, writing to seek brevet major rank, so the couple probably spent several years there. A few years later he purchased land on Grande Ile and there they lived until his death in 1806. An obelisk family monument stands in the yard of Trinity Anglican Church on the island, and their son Charles W. Grant, Baron de Longeuil, 1781-1848, is buried beneath it.

Grant had a partner in the land purchase. This was Lieutenant Patrick Langan of the KRRNY. The two officers had discovered that the Curot brothers, Amable and Michel, had acquired seigneurial title to the entire island, by descent from Jacques Cauchois, clerk of Sieur de LaSalle at Cataraqui. All subject to existing tenancies of course. Later the government of Upper Canada stepped in and took two-sevenths of the land for the crown and for clergy reserves. This still left plenty for the two soldiers, however, who had only wanted a couple of good farms in the first place.

In 1800 Lieutenant Langan complained to the Provincial Marine at Kingston about them cutting timber on the island, so he was still there. Maria, one of his three daughters, married the youngest son (Archie) of his old commanding officer, Colonel Sir John Johnson of the KRRNY who had built a fine house at Cataraqui after the war.

Enough whaleboats were completed in 1778 for a fall raid up the Oswego River. Then, in the winter, the artisans turned their hands to construction of three gunboats, each about sixty feet long, powered by thirty-six oarsmen and armed with a 12-pounder gun mounted in the bow. All were two-masted and two were lug-rigged. The third carried lateen sails, to perform better when close-hauled than her sisters. These row-galleys were intended to escort the bateaux brigades from Oswegatchie, a route now endangered by hostile, rebel-paid Oneidas, bands of whom were occasionally sighted along the river banks. The gunboat flotilla could also do great damage to any rebel force headed toward Carleton Island or Montreal by whaleboat. All three gunboats were completed by the spring of 1779. The next major project was the construction of *Ontario*.

Officer and Private and button of the 34th Foot, The Cumberland Regiment, c. 1778, parade-ground dress.

Upper left: Sloop Caldwell *from an unsigned drawing.*

Upper right: Unidentified topsail schooner at Niagara *c. 1780.*

Bottom: *In this view of Niagara the brig flies a commodore's pennant, so it could be Haldimand in 1779 or Ontario in 1780. She is docked at Navy Hall wharf on the west bank.*

The British vessels on Lake Ontario c. 1792.
Caldwell is the armed sloop in the centre. From a
painting by C.H.J. Snider.

A General Return of His Majesty's Armd Vessells &c. by Order of His Excellency

		Number of Vessels	Number of Guns	Number of Men	Vessells Names	Commanders Names
		1	16	34	Haldimand	James Andrews
Her Metal being too heavy I intend putting into her Sixpounders only and reduce the Number of Guns to fourteen		2	18	45	Seneca	Jn. Bte. Bouchette
		3	2	9	Caldwell	Wm. Baker
		4	4		Row Galley	
		5 & 6	2		Gun Batteaus	

A Return of Civil Officers and Men Employed in His

	Master Builder	Assistant Master Builder	Master Attendant	Assistant Master Attendant	Naval Storekeeper	Clerk to Naval Stores	Foreman of Shipwrights
	..	..	..	..	1	..	1

General Haldimand & S. & S. & c. under the direction of Captain John Schank Lake Ontario 1st January 1779

How Rigged	Length of Range Dck		Length of Keel for Tonnage		Breadth of the Beam		Depth of Hold		Height of Waste		Draught of Water fore / abft.		Tonnage	Quantity and Quality of Me								
	Feet	Inches	Feet	Inches	Feet	Inches	Feet	Inches	Feet	Inches	Feet Inches	Feet Inches	Tons	Pdr 24	Pdr 18	Pdr 12	Pdr 9	Pdr 6	Pdr 4	Pdr 3	Pdr 2	½ Pdr swivel
Snow														..	..	..	..	..	16	..	..	12
Snow	84	..	73	..	24	..	9	..	4	6	9.6	11		..	..	..	8	10	..	..	..	12
Sloop														..	..	..	..	..	2	..	..	..
Latten														..	..	4	..	..	..	..	..	..
Lugg														..	..	..	..	2	..	..	..	..
														..	..	4	8	12	18	..	..	24

Total of Gunns & Swivels Sixty Six

Majestys Dock Yard on Lake Ontario. 1st January 1779

Foreman of Sawyers	Foreman of H. Carpenters	Foreman of B. Smiths	Artificers & Labourers	Master Sailmaker & Crew	Boatswain of ye yard & Foreman of Riggers with his Crew	Surgeon	Officers Sick	Artificers Sick	Officers in Health	Artificers in Health
..	..	2	17	..	..	Wanted				

A *sketch of Schank Harbour.*
By Peter Rindlisbacher.

Building the Brig

THE MASTER SHIPWRIGHT posted to Lake Ontario was Mr. John Coleman, a professional trained at Royal Navy dockyards. He had worked with Lieutenant Schank in 1776 constructing the Lake Champlain vessels. In the fall of 1778 he was at Niagara repairing *Angelica* above the falls on Lake Erie and *Haldimand* at Niagara. On December 29th he received orders to start construction of a brig at Carleton Island, orders that Captain Schank had issued on October 30th.

A letter written by James Andrews, then captain of *Haldimand*, to his brother, Collin Andrews, a Detroit merchant, explains this delay, and speaks of other matters:

Navy Hall 12th Jan. 1779.

Dear Collin,-

We are very anxious to hear from your quarter, what is become of Governor Hamilton and where the three thousand Yankees got to. You may be equally desirous to hear from us, but we have very little new to send.

The Caldwell sloop winters at Carleton Island <u>by orders</u> to assist making a Pier. The Seneca after making several attempts and twice within a few Leagues of this Place, was obliged to put back the 14th of December and winter there. Also the 16th, Jacob Adam set out from there in a Battoe, left her at Toronto and arrived here the 29th with the Letters that were on Board the Seneca, all of an old date and contain no material news. * * * *

No late news from England. Mr. Coleman received orders from Capt. Schank, dated the 30th of October, to build a new vessel this year. The dock yard was to be established at Carleton Island. Therefore he was to cut no more timber, nor prepare any more materials than sufficient to finish the work then in hand at Niagara, but as these orders did not arrive until the 29th of December, all that is left for Mr. Coleman is to repair the Haldimand and Angelica and cut crooked timber, saw oak and pine, to carry down with us in the spring, but I am certainly sorry that all these matters go on very slowly, and although I have no command over the ship carpenters, only to assist the master builder, yet I have much reason to expect that great part of the blame will be laid at my door, whereas in reality the fault lies in Capt. S., not being acquainted with this service and too opinionated to consult with those who are. I have had two letters from him and the general tenor of his former orders contain little than for me to assist Mr. Coleman on the public works. He is pleased to congratulate me on the General's having appointed me to command on Lake Ontario, the same as Capt. Chambers and Grant on the other Lakes, but as I have no Commission and as Col. Bolton's wary Disposition, although much my Friend, will not advance my Pay, I cannot look on myself as on a level with them. Enclosed I send you a copy of Gen. Haldimand's orders to Col. Bolton respecting me, and I am sorry to say the words ''I consider'' do not convey the force of an order. However, I must make the best I can of it, and try every means in my power to obtain the commission. Colonel Bolton has written twice strongly recommending me. On his Application I have great Hopes and I have thought of writing to Colonel Claus, who I believe has good interest at Head quarters. The unsettled situation of my own Affairs with the removal of our Headquarters to Carleton Island, puts it out of my power to give any Advice about your removal to this place. * * * *

John Schank, "Admiral of the Blue," in his later years. He served in Canada from 1776 to 1784.

Mrs. Andrews and family all in good health send their respectful
Compliments,
I remain dear Collin,

> *Your affect. brother,*
> *James Andrews.*

To Mr. Collin Andrews.
  Merchant, Detroit.

The carpenter foreman, John Clunes, who was also shipyard clerk, had come to Canada from Britain in March 1776 as one of about sixty carpenters and artificers sent out to build armed vessels on Lake Champlain. One of his travelling companions in the transport *Speke* was Francis Goring, a young man who went to Niagara to work for the merchant James Robinson. The two kept up a correspondence between Carleton Island and Fort Niagara. Clunes apparently had a poor opinion of Captain Aubrey, the commandant, as may be seen from two of his letters:

To Mr. Goring

> *Carleton Island March 24th 1779*

Sir.

> *Very agreeably I received your letter dated Decr 1st., which did afford me great satisfaction to hear of your agreeable situation. About a Month before I left you I was made a Master Sawyer at the pay of 4. st'g per day and remain at that pay still. * * * **
I came to this place along with the Commanding Engineer, Lieut. Wil'm Twiss, who is my friend. I am in a very good place and have made several friends to myself by my sobriety and attention to my duty I have keep't my health in this

Drawings from an old text on shipbuilding, showing how knees and futtocks are visualized in live trees.

country very well. * * * * This Garrison is very near finished and I may venture is the strongest place in NORTH AMERICA. I hope it will be an honor to our Engineer and a credit to our Master Carpenter and me, and every Artificier concerned in building it. The Commanding Off'r of this place has quarreled with every officer in this place except Mr. Baker Capt. Anderson and Gill the doctor so that no officer will speak to him. I return you my hearty thanks for your useful and generous present of Potatoes, and depend if it ever lays in my power to serve you I will. I hope that you will excuse my long letter and I hope you will write me as soon as possible and you will much oblige your,

Ob't Humble Serv't
John Clunes
Clerk and Foreman

Carleton Island March 25th 1779

To Mr. Goring.

Sir.

* * * * * I wrote to you a small epistle of my life since I parted with you, but were we to meet I would surprise you to tell you of some things, and make you Laugh at Others. I mean in regard to Men that come out with us, both Artificiers and salors.

Last night Doctor Gill, got _____ _____ Kicked in company by Mr. Morrison, a Merch't, upon which insted of resenting it went to the Commanding Officer and told the Commanding Officer that he was in Dangour of his life, upon which he swore his life against Morrison, and ever since Morrison has had a soldier after him day and night, but gets leave to walk about, and is a prisoner at large. In this Confusion has the Garrison been in, all *this winter and no Officer keeps the Commandants' company, scarce, except a certain Watery Hero, and a piddlen prattling Surgeon's Mate who stiles himself a Doctor, and says he is a very good one if he had drugges but being so much engaged with the Beautys of this Island and almost every night drunk, forgot to send in due season to Canada for drugges, so that three parts out of four of the men is sick with the scurvy and _____ other sicknesses. * * * * **

I remain your friend and well wisher,
John Clunes
Clerk and Foreman

"The Beauty's of this Island" later included some of Molly Brant's six daughters, one of whom, Elizabeth, did marry a Carleton Island doctor named Robert Kerr, not James deCourcy Gill. (Sir William Johnson, in his will, referred to Molly as "My housekeeper Mary Brant, the mother of eight of my children." Captain Andrews called her "Miss Molly Johnson" and the daughters used the Johnson surname.)

During the winter of 1778-79 timber was selected and cut for two larger vessels. White oak was the favoured tree, but very few grew nearby with any length of trunk. Red oak, in contrast, was plentiful in groves along the river, soaring 30 or 40 feet before branching out, almost like pine. To build a brig, John Coleman, the master shipwright, preferred white oak for all the major timbers but would take what was within reach. Although he had learned his trade in England, he had great respect for the skills of the French-Canadian artisans who worked in the shipyards at Sorel. Several of these were in his labour force. Their foreman spent many days on long tramps through the woods bordering the river to seek out oaks with suitable curve or "compass" naturally grown. Big timbers could be bent after a long period in the steam box, but time was a major factor, and a naturally curved timber was therefore preferred. Throughout the winter the selected trees were felled, hewn roughly square, and hauled on bob-sleighs over the frozen river to the yard. The curved trees

Private and Officer and button of the 84th Foot, The Royal Highland Emigrants, c. 1778, in full dress. Note the thistles on the button.

were needed for many special applications such as the stem and the frames or ribs. Even maple, beech, white ash, or elm, if curved, were cut and stockpiled. Work parties from the 47th and the KRRNY did the rough felling, limbing, and dragging to the ice. The final square-hewing and tapering was left to be done in the spring, after completion of work on the three galleys.

A wharf and break-water was needed to protect Schank Harbour from north west winds. Somehow time was found to build the timber cribs on the ice. These were then sunk and filled with rocks. Local divers report that some of the oak wharf timbers are still in good shape after two centuries submerged in the St. Lawrence River, a good indication of the life expectancy of *Ontario's* hull.

For better protection of the new vessel on the stocks and of the naval barracks which lay on the low ground between the coves, a block house was built in the fall of 1779. This stood on the westerly point, with fields of fire for its three guns, designed to cover both of the coves.

The arrival of the second battalion of the 84th Foot, The Royal Highland Emigrants, helped solve the labour shortage while increasing security. These were older men, many of whom had taken up soldier's land grants in Canada at the conclusion of General Wolfe's campaign. Members of Fraser's Highlanders, turned into Canadian farmers, they were handy with axe and hammer as well as musket or broadsword. (Fraser's Highlanders, the 78th Regiment, was raised at Inverness in 1758 for service in North America. It was disbanded in Canada in 1763.) On parade they wore the green government sett kilt, racoon-skin sporrans, and blue facings on their scarlet tunics. Off parade they wore loose white trousers and short black gaiters as protection against summer blackflies and winter cold. As former "Jacobites" or supporters of Prince Charles Stuart, some flaunted the white cockade, a Jacobite badge, on their bonnets. "The White Cockade" was also a popular tune with their fifers and fiddlers.

The Americans were well aware of the activity at Carleton, as indicated in

THE WHITE COCKADE   Carr, *Evening Amusement*

a letter from Sgt-Major James Clark of the 8th King's Regiment, who had been posted from Niagara and given his discharge to act as Naval Storekeeper. After the war Clark settled at Cataraqui, then moved to Napanee. His first two children were born on Carleton Island, so his wife obviously lived there too. In June 1779, Clark wrote to Mr. F. Goring concerning enemy activity on the island:

To Mr. F. Goring, Niagara

Carleton Island 10th June 1779

Sir,

By the return of the Seneca, you will please sent me two Quires of your largest Paper and charge it to the Naval Department. I am safe at Carleton Island, but not yet so well situated as I would wish.

We are repeatedly alarmed by the Enemy's scouts, who, a few days ago, took away two men from the Island, not one hundred yards from the Fort, and at ten o'clock in the morning. Up the whole of last night by alarms.

I am, Sir, Yours & c.,
James Clark

Throughout the summer of 1779 Haldimand, under Captain James Andrews, shuttled back and forth on the lake and the river. "Crooked timber" gathered at Niagara was carried down to Carleton for knees. Packs of furs, some belonging to Andrews' brother, were loaded for shipment east along with "Miss Molly Johnson, her retinue, prisoners, Loyalists, horses, and the Lord knows what else," as the captain put it in the letter of July 19th 1779 to his brother Collin. He bought oats to feed the horses but had a hard time convincing the Naval Department that a vessel required oats. A considerable number of horses were in use at the long Niagara portage, probably purchased from local Seneca farmers. The need for draft animals was great at Fort Haldimand, hence the shipment. The wording of his commission as Commodore of Lake Ontario vessels seems to have lacked something, causing him difficulties, as he explained to his brother in this letter:

Private of the grenadier company and Officer of the 8th Foot, The King's Regiment. Other styles of button have been found as well.

Niagara 16th July 1779.

Dear Collin,-

This will be delivered to you by Mr. Robertson, Clerk of the Cheque for the Naval Dept., a very genteel young man, and whom as being a stranger, I earnestly request you will please to show civilities particularly, if anyways convenient, to give him a room in your house for the few days he may stay. Capt. Schank will, I suppose, be accommodated by Capt. Lemoult, but if not, I hope you will be able to spare them two rooms. Lieut. Harrow who accompanies these gentlemen, served time with me in the Haldimand. To him also I request you will show civilities. **** The remainder of your Packs I am now taking on Board and Sail tomorrow with Mrs. Hay, your old Acquaintance Miss Molly Johnson and Retinue, Prisoners, Loyalists, Horses and the Lord knows what else. I fear much you think very oddly of me this Spring. The truth is Collin, I have met with such *a variety of untoward Accidents and have had so much active Service, that I have not had time to attend to anything relative to myself or anyway's belonging to me, and moreover the Changes talked of in our Department, has latterly entirely unhinged me. How they are to be settled I know not, but it seems to me they are trying every possible Means to get quit of me, and to give this Lake up to Capt. Laforce and Canadians. However, I understand the final Arrangement is to be settled between Capt. Brehm and Capt. Schank, therefore, probably you may hear of it before I shall. Among my other Crosses and Lapses at this place, I have lost Snow. He's gone off with the Indians. I wish to write Capt. Grant, Betton and Burnette, to whom I am indebted letters, but in the present State of Affairs I am utterly at a loss how to address them. A Quire of Paper in my irregular rig-me-roll writing would not explain to them the Cause of my long Silence. Should Capt. Grant think that I have had any hand in manufacturing the Charges talked of, will do me very great Injustice and I hope time will prove that Justice to show all these matters in their proper colour, As I do not propose writing to him now I beg you will speak to him on this Subject, also to thank Betton for his last letter which I shall answer I hope on my return with English news.*

Mrs. Andrews and family all in good health send their respectful Compliments. I remain dear Collin,

Your affect. brother,
James Andrews.

Please send my Acct. The price of the Oats I want, much as I must, Charge them to the Dept. Acct.

To Mr. Collin Andrews, Merchant, Detroit.

When the work began in earnest on the new brig in the early autumn of 1779, the civilian work force consisted of sixty-nine men, namely the Master Builder

(John Coleman), Naval Storekeeper (James Clark), Foreman of Shipwrights (John Clunes), Foreman of Blacksmiths, Bo's'n of the Yard, Surgeon (James Gill), and sixty-three artificers of various special categories. "Charcoal burners" were included in the list of these tradesmen; presumably the blacksmiths relied on charcoal to operate their forges. "Tar-maker" was a somewhat more puzzling description for an occupation; perhaps the resin of the local pitch and red pines was distilled to produce both turpentine and Stockholm tar. The pitch-pine is fairly common in the Thousand Islands, by strange coincidence one of two small areas where it grows in Canada. Most tar used by the Royal Navy was purchased in Sweden, Russia, and other Baltic countries with coniferous forests. In this case it was much cheaper and simpler to make it on the spot. The boilers used to generate steam for the steam-boxes only needed a coil of copper pipe to convert them into stills. Tar and turpentine were made by distilling bark and branches of resinous trees.

Another specialist, the Cooper, made buckets, tubs, and barrels, including many tar barrels (an accidental fire in the naval stores destroyed a large number). The ideal wood for making barrel hoops was the local black ash, also known as hoop ash. When heated, it bends easily and stays bent. The Mohawk also used it for snowshoe frames, canoe ribs, and baskets. Small ash logs were soaked in the river and left to freeze in the ice, held down by flat stones. In spring the annular rings could be easily separated into thin, pliable strips for weaving baskets of many styles and sizes.

The Joiner produced such items as the binnacle, the booby-hatch over the officers ladderway, the skylight, the stern windows, the quarter-galleries, and panelling in the captain's quarters. Black walnut, available from Niagara, was a suitable wood for built-in desk and drawers. Walnut also made good gratings, but they were very heavy, unless framed in cedar. The combination floated, as it turned out.

The Naval Storekeeper held a most important post. The smooth progress

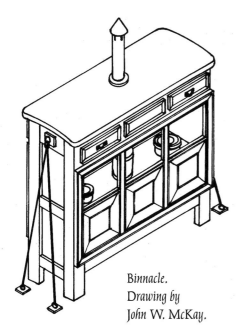

Binnacle.
Drawing by
John W. McKay.

of construction in the yard was dependent on the availability of a wide range of materials, many of which had to be ordered from far-off Quebec City. Because of the long delivery time, such needs had to be anticipated well in advance. James Clark was responsible for supply, but of course depended on John Coleman to keep him provided with a "want list" looking months ahead.

Clark was Battalion Sergeant Major of the 8th Foot, stationed at Niagara in 1778. Because the regiment was scattered over several forts on the lakes his duties were not the usual ones. Colonel Masson Bolton, his C.O., felt he could be more effectively employed as storekeeper at Carleton Island, and gave him his discharge from the army along with the nice civilian job. It happened that the 8th lost both their adjutant and quartermaster at Niagara about then. No officers wanted these postings, so Bolton gave commissions as lieutenants to his quartermaster sergeant and orderly room sergeant forthwith. Perhaps having two of his friends move to the officer's mess induced Clark to take the job at Carleton.

Under James Clark the naval stores did a brisk business satisfying the needs of the four active ships on Lake Ontario. Now they started to bulge with the wide and varied inventory built up to supply the new *Ontario*. General Haldimand received extensive returns signed by Captain Schank as Commissioner and William Robertson "Clerk of the Cheque" headed "A Return of all ye Naval Stores at the different Dockyards Viz: Quebec, Niagara, Carleton Island etc." Items included "Musquets, French; Musquets Bright Black English; Slings for ditto; Pistols, paires; Blunderbuses; Cutlasses; Swords; Common Locks for 6 pdr cannon; Flints; Balles; Quires of Paper for Cartridges; Copper Powder Measures; Tin ditto; Glasses, Watch, 14 Seconds, 28 Seconds, 1/2 Hour, 1 Hour, 2 Hour; Stone Ground Panes; Paint, Red, Kegs; White, lbs., Yellow, lbs., Linseed Oil, gallons; ditto Barrels; Sweet Oil, quarts; Glue; Chalk; Oars, Boat Hooks, Handspikes; Blocks (13 types); Dead Eyes (3

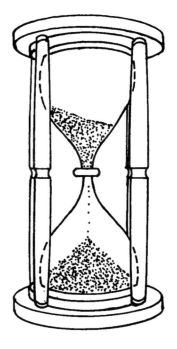

Hourglass.
Drawing by John W. McKay.

Adze.

sizes); Brushes, Tarr; Scrubbing ditto; Moppes, Cabbin; Kneedles, Roping & Sail; Palm Irons; Lanthornes, hand; Grindstones, Sharping Stones, Leather Buckets; Sails (at least 32 kinds from Small Jibbs to Trysails); Tarr, Barrells; Pitch, Barrells; Turpentine ditto; Varnish of Pine, gallons; Brimstone, Tallow, Kegs; Lampblack, ditto; Irons, Caulking; Mallets, ditto; Mauls, Ditto; Gimblets; Augurs; Rules; Chizels; Saws; Mill, Whip, X cut, Hand; files; Hinges, Cupboard; Brass Knobs for Doors; Kettles copper; ditto Brass; ditto Tin; Ships Bells; Compasses, Brass; ditto Wood; Spare Cards ditto; Glasses for ditto; Nails (a dozen sizes, including shingle and brads) Bunting, Yds. Red, yds. White; Shalloons, yards (wool cloth used for signal flags and gunpowder charge bags) White, Red, Blue, Yellow; Hammac cord; Oil Cloaths; Anchors, Iron stocked, Wood ditto, Grapnels; Broad Axes, Pole ditto, Felling ditto; Iron Crows, Shovels; Tongs; Ballast Shovels; Scrapers; Fish Hooks; Chain Bolts; Ring Bolts; Iron Chains Five Fathoms Each; Roasting Spits; Iron Pottes; Canthooks; Tackle Hooks; Fidd Hammers; Iron Fidds; Iron Hanks; Marline Spikes; Iron Wedges; Adzes

Flat Iron, lbs; Bolt Iron, lbs.; Rod Iron Washers; Steel, lbs; Loggerheads (tool for melting pitch); Creepers; Thimbles; Sheets of Tin; Hand Leads; Spare Foot of ditto; deepsea Leads; Lead Lines; deepsea Lines; Logglines; Hambro Lines; Marline, white, skeins; Whiterope Coils; Chalk lines; Twine, lbs.; ditto damage; Spunyarn Coils; Old Rigging, lbs.; Canvas, bolts No.'s 1,2,3,4,5,6,7 and 8; Fearnought, yards (protective cloth for powder magazine)."

The lists are hard to read because of fading, quaint spelling, and some indecipherable writing. The above sample, although incomplete, gives a good idea of the materials held. The "red and white bunting" was probably used to decorate *Ontario* for her launching. "Bright, Black English Musquets" are, of course, Brown Bess flintlocks. "French Musquets" are also mentioned, obviously captured in 1760. No locks are listed for any cannon except for the 6-pounder. Possibly the 4-pounders were touched off with a port-fire match, and perhaps the charge-bags were made from different coloured cloth for each calibre. If so, less chance of a dangerous mix-up between 6-pounder and 4-pounder. "Stone-ground panes" do not sound like clear glass. Perhaps they were used in the "Lanthornes" or were they intended for use in windows and skylights where privacy was desired?

The thousands of treenails or 'trunnels' needed were roughly split to size and finished on a bow lathe, foot-powered. This work was probably contracted out to local oar-makers who for many years had supplied the bateaux requirements of white ash oars and iron-shod 'perch poles' (a perch is 16 1/2 feet). Hickory and ironwood made strong treenails, but the best material was black locust, which is now common around the Cataraqui River. If it was introduced there by the French ship-builders in the seventeenth century, then it was available to Mr. Coleman, locally.

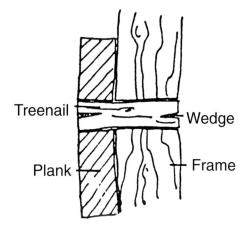

*H*aving just come down from making repairs to *Haldimand* and *Angelica* at Niagara, John Coleman was very conscious of the hazards surrounding lake navigation. He knew also that his vessel had a life expectancy of, at best, seven to ten years, and that speedy completion was critical because the old *Haldimand* could not hold together much longer. Timber was cheap, plentiful, and massive — a great change from Britain's shipyards. Therefore he framed his vessel on the robust side, subordinating neatness to strength, when time could be saved thereby and sturdiness ensured. This hull must withstand the pressure of winter ice every year and the grinding of ice-floes every spring, things of which her Admiralty designers never dreamt. Running aground in the river and its approaches would be a common event. There is no tide to simplify careening when keel or bottom damage requires repair, so Coleman availed himself of the ready supply of primeval oak trees and built her a little on the coarse side, a draft horse rather than a thoroughbred, but completed on time. With a length-to-breadth ratio of 3.16 to 1, she was quite "tubby" by design.

In addition to the timber for the new brig cut locally, the water-powered saw-mills at Niagara and Oswegatchie produced pine and oak plank at a fraction of the labour required in the saw-pits on the island. Hand-sawing a log into planks requires two men and a pit. The man in the pit must cope with a constant rain of sawdust into his eyes and nose, very unpopular work and also very slow. A raised platform can usually be used for sawing smaller pieces, and this lets the breeze take care of the sawdust.

A few miles east of Carleton Island on the south shore of the St. Lawrence River, "Saw Mill Creek" empties into the river. Whether a saw mill was set up there during the Revolution or not until later settlement has not been determined. For winter use, sawn lumber could have been transported across the ice to the yard with ease. Navigation was closed from freeze-up until April, cutting off supplies from Oswegatchie and Niagara. It is just possible that the engineers did set up saw mill machinery on this convenient creek, although defence would be a concern.

Pit-sawing was still necessary for many special operations when axe and adze hewing was too rough. Many of the lodging knees, which brace the deck beams horizontally, were cut out of pine root and stump by a combination of axe and saw. Other knees were made from oak branches. Oak grown in a natural curve was preferable, but curved members could be patterned onto a wide slab sawn out of a tree trunk and then hewn to shape. Oak plank used for wales could be softened and bent after a soak in boiling water or a steam box. The steam box had been in use for boat building by the Royal Navy since 1736. A wooden trough, kept filled from a battery of cauldrons supplied the need but, again, much labour was required to bail water back and forth. After steaming or

Foot-powered treadle lathe, on display at the MacLachlan Woodworking Museum, Kingston, Ontario. Note stone flywheel.

soaking, massive iron "C" clamps drew the pliable planks into place, where they were bolted and treenailed securely. To simplify the curving process, a bending frame or hickey was sometimes employed. Adjustable cross-bars held down one end of a hot, steam-softened wale, while it was bent over several other bars by the weight of a box of rocks on the free end. Green oak, still full of sap, was the easiest to shape.

John Coleman kept a list of timbers brought to the yard. Each was numbered and noted for species, length, diameter, and curvature. When the snow was gone in spring 1779, his carpenters planked a framing platform upon which to lay out the lines full size for each of the fifty ribs or frames of the vessel. The draught plan from the Admiralty gave these exactly. A six-inch grid painted on the floor assisted in the transfer and a shed roof protected workers from sun and rain. A pattern for each frame was carefully cut out from thin pine to be used in shaping the thick oak sections. These were clearly labelled and stored for later use in the construction of *Limnade*, the sister vessel of *Ontario*. ("Lymniad" means water-sprite, so this is probably a spelling variation.) Meanwhile, the keel was assembled from two massive oak timbers joined by a scarf joint 10 feet in overlap, and pinned with a dozen black locust tenons or treenails. An iron pin was driven vertically through each end of the joint and a pair of iron fish-plates were bolted through the overlap from side to side near each pin, neatly recessed into the wood. At the fore end of the keel, another scarf joint connected it to the curved stem, similarly reinforced.

The stern post was a straight timber rising at a steep angle from the keel and attached by a wood knee cut from the bole and a large branch of a carefully chosen oak. Again iron bolts and treenails were employed and a pair of fish plates bolted through the foot of the post and the end of the keel.

Each frame (or rib) was shaped and fitted on the platform from its nine segments, double thick — four pieces one side, five on the other, with joints

Shipbuilding.

staggered. First erected was the largest or midship frame at the widest point in the hull. This was 25 feet 4 inches wide and 16 feet high. The bottom section or floor which spanned the keel was 11 inches deep by 11 inches across. The frames tapered up from the keel, with the top timbers or upper futtocks about 8 inches by 6. The two layers of each frame were fastened together with treenails and iron bolts. The floor timber was notched into the keel 2 inches (1 inch cut from the keel, 1 inch from the floor). An iron bolt was driven through each floor into the keel.

When all the frames were in place and secured by temporary horizontal wales, the keelson was lowered in. This was the second largest member, running from the stem to the sternpost knee over the frames and notched into them. Long scarf joints again connected the three segments. The centre section was placed over the joint in the keel for added strength. At every second frame, a 1 1/2 inch iron bolt was driven down through the keelson, the floor frame and the keel — a very long hole to drill with a hand auger, as at the midship frame the keelson was 15 inches wide by 12 inches deep and the keel was 15 inches by 18 inches deep. Both timbers tapered at bow and stern to match the thinner vertical members.

At this point in construction, all frames were notched from below on each side of the keel to allow bilge water to flow to the pumps. Also a rabbet was cut into each side of the keel to accept the first plank or garboard strake. At the scarf joints in the keel and stem, a hole was drilled horizontally through the seam just below the rabbet and plugged with a dowel to stop water following the joint up inside.

The mast steps were two large blocks of oak bolted through the keelson to the keel with four bolts each. A knee on each side braced the steps against adjoining frames.

Frames at the bow were notched into the stem and backed with a timber called the apron. Where the hull swooped up astern, emulating the shape of a

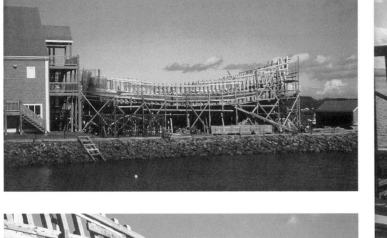

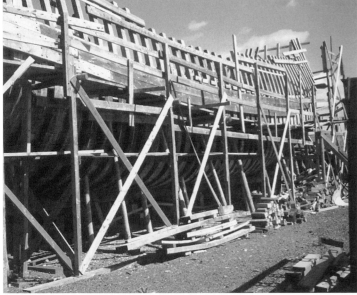

Hector *under construction at Pictou, Nova Scotia by* The Hector Foundation. *The original* Hector *was of similar size and vintage as* Ontario.

Upper: A frame or hickey for bending steam-softened wales to be used in Hector.

Lower: A pile of "crooked timber" for her shipwrights.

Caulking mallet (top) and various augers (below), on display at the MacLachlan Woodworking Museum.

fish, additional deadwood timbers filled in the triangle leading to the stern post. Four long iron gudgeons served as reinforcing straps on each side, bolted through post, knee, and deadwood. The crotch in each gudgeon contained a 2 1/2 inch hole for a rudder pintle.

To connect the frames and support the lower or gun deck, a massive horizontal timber called the shelf clamp or simply clamp, was bolted to the frames along each side of the vessel. Because the clamp was composed of several segments, scarf joints again came into play. Curvature at the bow made this a difficult timber to fit accurately, and required a number of good, naturally curved members.

On the clamp rested the 13 gundeck beams, each 14 inches wide by 12 inches deep and about 5 foot 6 inches on centre. Each beam was notched 4 inches into the clamp. The clamp itself was 12 inches deep by 8 inches wide to allow for this. Above the deck-beam ends came another longitudinal timber called the waterway, 8 inches deep by 8 inches, notched down 2 inches for each beam. A 1 1/4 inch iron bolt was driven down through waterway, beam, and clamp to tie all together at every beam. Each deck beam was cambered up 5 inches for drainage and to provide a little slope to ease the run-out of the guns. Below them at the mid-point ran an 8 inch by 12 inch lengthwise supporting timber resting on 7 inch posts or pillars, which, in turn, sat on the keelson.

White oak knees reinforced the junction of the stem and both length-wise timbers as well as the transom beams at the stern. Iron hanging knees made by the St. Maurice foundry and forge at Trois Rivieres tied each deck beam to a corresponding frame, both port and starboard. While rather heavy and expensive, iron knees were stronger, saved considerable time, and had been in limited use in Quebec yards since at least 1750.

This construction might be overly sturdy for a cargo brig, but one must remember that the lower deck would carry fourteen 6-pounder guns, each weighing, with carriage and ready shot, a ton, plus crew. The frame must also withstand the shock of firing a full broadside of nine guns at one time and be capable of surviving many hits by enemy guns before disintegrating. In a bad storm, strains even beyond any to be expected in battle would arise, and grounding, a common accident on the lakes, could break the back of an unlucky victim. In northern waters respect must be shown for the winter-long pressure of ice, sometimes wind-driven with enormous force, capable of crushing light vessels into kindling.

Planking started next, mostly 2 1/2 inch pine from the sawmills, carefully fitted and treenailed to every frame. A wedge driven into a sawcut spread the head of each treenail and held it tight. Above the waterline, heavier planking was used to stop musket balls and shot, especially at the swell of the sides. Here, at the widest part of each frame, a 6 inch thick oak plank or wale was placed to withstand the bumps of a wharf or another vessel alongside. This wale was bolted through to the clamp.

The frames still projected upward 6 feet above the gun deck to allow for the upper deck, called quarterdeck aft, and 'fo'c's'le' forward. This was carried on twenty-one beams, each 9 by 6 inches at 4 foot 6 inch centres supported by another clamp and held down by another waterway somewhat lighter than those below. Headroom in the gun deck was 6 feet aft in the officer cabins and 5 foot 6 inches in the fo'c's'le and the waist. Both decks were planked with white pine nailed down.

The draught clearly shows deck beams for the upper deck over the waist. It was common practise to plank a narrow gangway along each side over the guns and to leave the centre area about 14 feet wide by 24 long open to allow smoke from the guns to dissipate during battle. The beams carried spare spars and the boats. Because of the frequent need for additional passenger and crew accommodation under cover, temporary light pine decking could be lashed to the beams over the open waist area. A tarpaulin stretched from gangway to gangway kept out the rain.

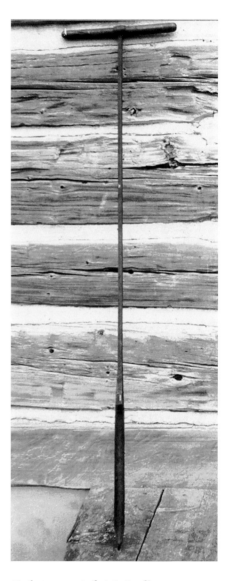

Six-foot auger, at the MacLachlan Woodworking Museum.

Inset in the stern were six casement windows and on each side, close to the stern, was a projecting bay window called a quarter gallery. One of these was designed as a toilet for the officers. Within, the commander's quarters were fairly spacious and well lit, although encumbered with 6-pounder guns port and starboard.

The inner planking or ceiling was installed next. In wooden ships the ceiling has nothing to do with the underside of the deck over head, which is called the deckhead, but constitutes the lining of the hull. Planks of 2 inch pine served here, fastened with nails except those close to the keelson which were left loose for cleaning out bilge gunk. Below the waterline, a 3 inch space was left between each ceiling plank to permit the circulation of air and thus retard dry rot.

Sixteen gun ports, each 2 feet 6 inches wide by 2 feet high at 9 foot 6 inch centres, were cut through the gun deck sides, framed, and fitted with hinged covers. Two more 2 foot square transom ports were cut in the stern just below the gun deck, possibly to accommodate a pair of 1/2-pounder swivel guns. These could be mounted on the small raised platform in the after part of the hold, just above the water line, on occasion.

Ballast guns from hulks in Deadman Bay. Note the trunnion still on the horizontal gun with the exploded breech.

In the fore part of the hold, another partial deck served as the galley, various storage lockers, and cabins for petty officers. Wooden gratings over all hatches allowed some air and light to reach every part of the ship. Solid wood hatch covers were reserved for stormy weather and winter.

Ballast consisted in part of tarred sacks of shingle, stowed on both sides of the keelson. About three hundred iron shot and two hundred canisters in wooden cases of eight each helped in the ballast calculation. These were carried in a shot locker just ahead of the mainmast. The ready-use shot was set in garlands gouged out of the top of the waterway between guns and also out of the main hatch coaming (where, in action, it could be replenished from the hold). Additional iron ballast was found at Fort Frontenac in the form of old French guns "de-trunnioned" and spiked by Lieut. Col. John Bradstreet twenty years previously. Many of these lay about the old fort, too heavy to steal. Six of the heaviest were selected and taken by sleigh to Carleton to await the launching. Other ballast guns from Fort Frontenac were still in use in 1815. Some recovered from scuttled vessels in Deadman Bay are displayed at Fort Henry. Real veterans, they have probably served as ballast in a succession of lake vessels, moving on as each wore out and was condemned. The ballast was not removed from the Deadman Bay frigates as by then (c.1840) iron pigs were cheaply available, and much more practical. In 1807 when the last British caretakers were withdrawn from Fort Haldimand, the few remaining guns on the island were sunk in deep water by order of Captain Andrew Gray, commandant of the re-located dockyard at Point Frederick, Kingston. Evidently the need for old cannon had passed, although some were used as bollards on the government pier and others at the gate to protect its stonework from wagon wheel hubs. One pair still stands at the RMC guardroom.

Condemned guns at the Royal Military College inner gate.

Stone ballast also waited on the wharf, with the spars and guns, for the big moment in the spring of 1780 when the ice would be gone and the water level of the river risen sufficiently to enable the launching of *Ontario*.

Drawings of *Ontario*
by JOHN W. MCKAY
based on the
Admiralty Draught of 1780.

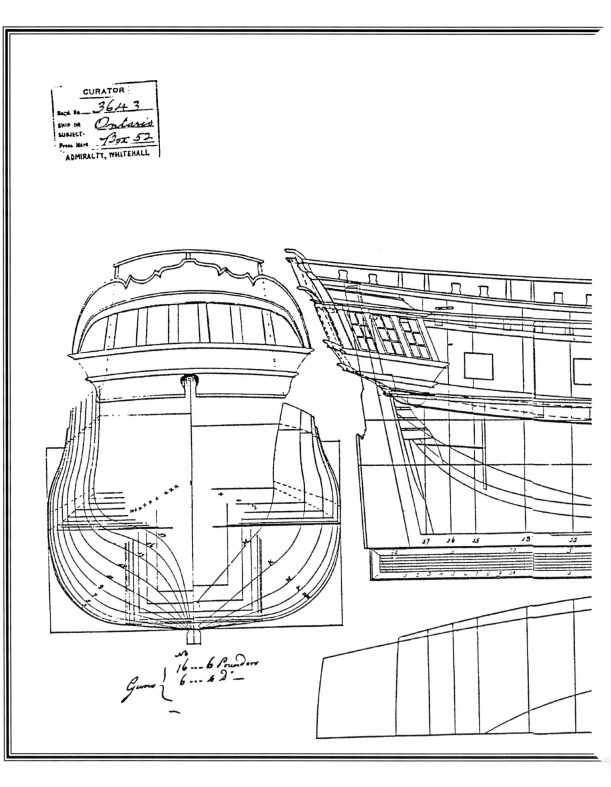

Guns { 16 ... 6 Pounders
6 ... 4 D°

A Draught of the Ontario Launch'd at Carleton Island the 10 May 1780

Feet In
Length on the Lower Deck ———— 80 — 0
Of the Keel for Tonage ———— 64 — 0 ¾
Breadth Extream ———— 25 — 4
Depth in Hold ———— 9 — 0
Burthen in Tons ———— 226 55/94

P.S. Carleton Island is in Lake Ontario about 154 Miles N.E. of Niagara

Richman

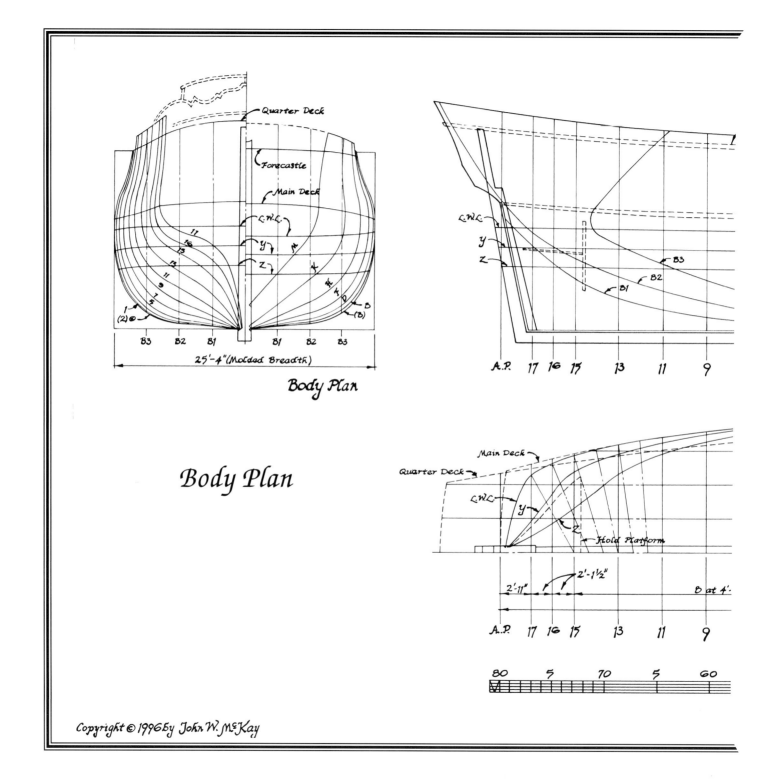

Quarter Deck

Forecastle

Main Deck

C.W.C.

y

z

B3   B2   B1   B1   B2   B3

25'-4"(Molded Breadth)

Body Plan

Body Plan

C.W.C.

y

z

B3

B2

B1

A.P.   17 16 15   13   11   9

Main Deck

Quarter Deck

C.W.C.

y

z

Hold Platform

2'-11"   2'-1½"   D at 4'-

A.P.   17 16 15   13   11   9

80   5   70   5   60

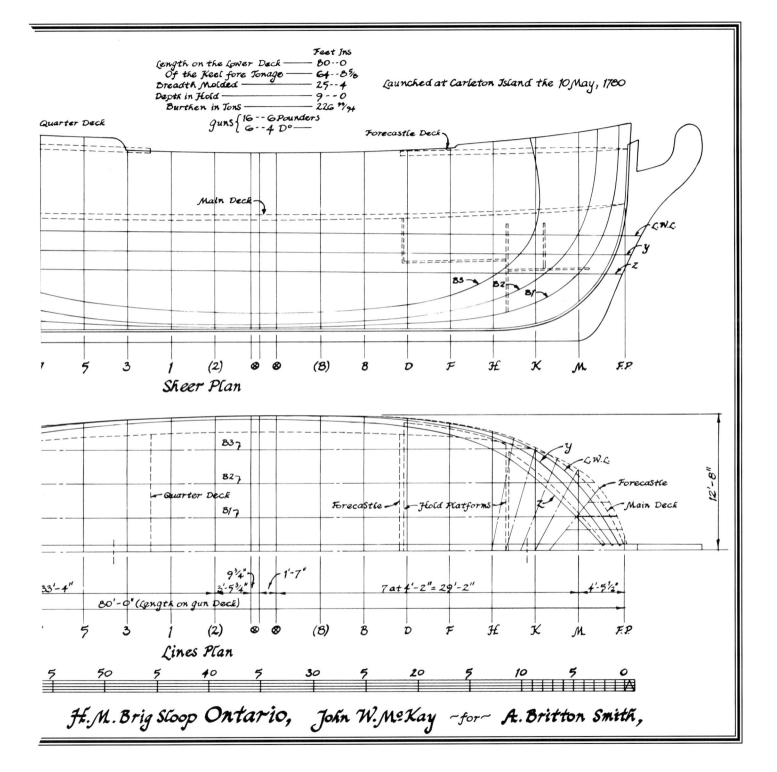

	Feet Ins
Length on the Lower Deck	80--0
Of the Keel fore Tonage	64--8⅝
Breadth Molded	25--4
Depth in Hold	9--0
Burthen in Tons	226 ⁴⁹/₉₄

guns { 16 -- 6 Pounders / 6 -- 4 D°

Launched at Carleton Island the 10 May, 1780

Quarter Deck

Forecastle Deck

Main Deck

L.W.L.
y
z

B3   B2   B1

5   3   1   (2)   ⊗ ⊗   (8)   8   D   F   H   K   M   F.P.

Sheer Plan

B3
B2
Quarter Deck
B1

Forecastle   Hold Platforms

y
L.W.L.
Forecastle
z
Main Deck

12'-8"

33'-4"

9¾"   1'-7"
2'-5¾"   7 at 4'-2" = 29'-2"   4'-5½"

80'-0" (length on gun Deck)

5   3   1   (2)   ⊗ ⊗   (8)   B   D   F   H   K   M   F.P.

Lines Plan

5 50 5 40 5 30 5 20 5 10 5 0

H.M. Brig Sloop Ontario,   John W. McKay ~for~ A. Britton Smith,

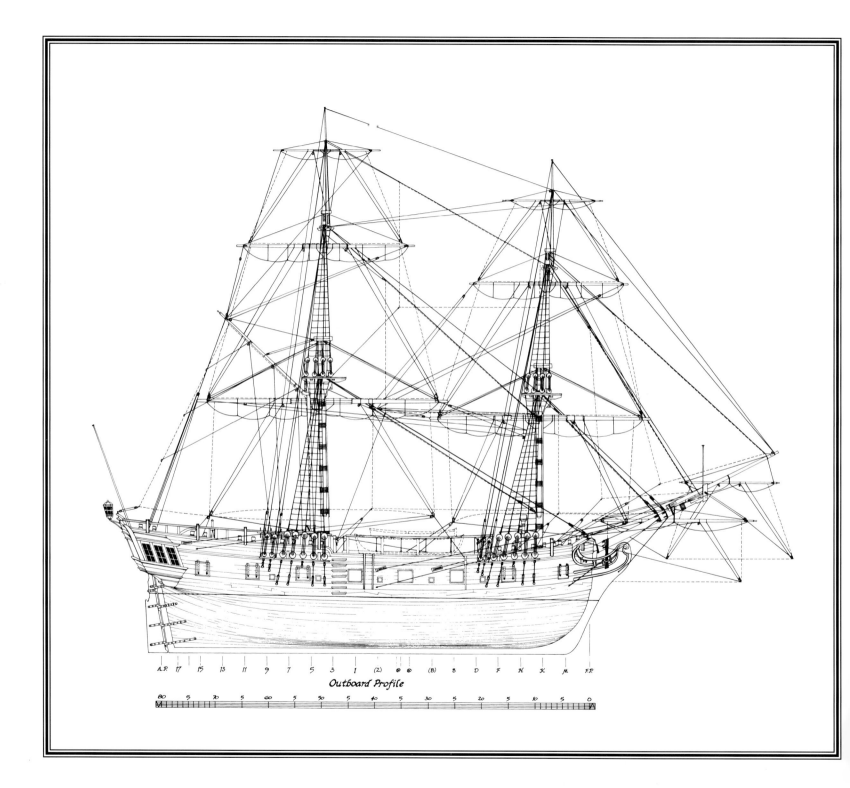

A.P. 17 15 13 11 9 7 5 3 1 (2) ⊗⊗ (B) B D F H K M F.P.

Outboard Profile

80 5 70 5 60 5 50 5 40 5 30 5 20 5 10 5 0

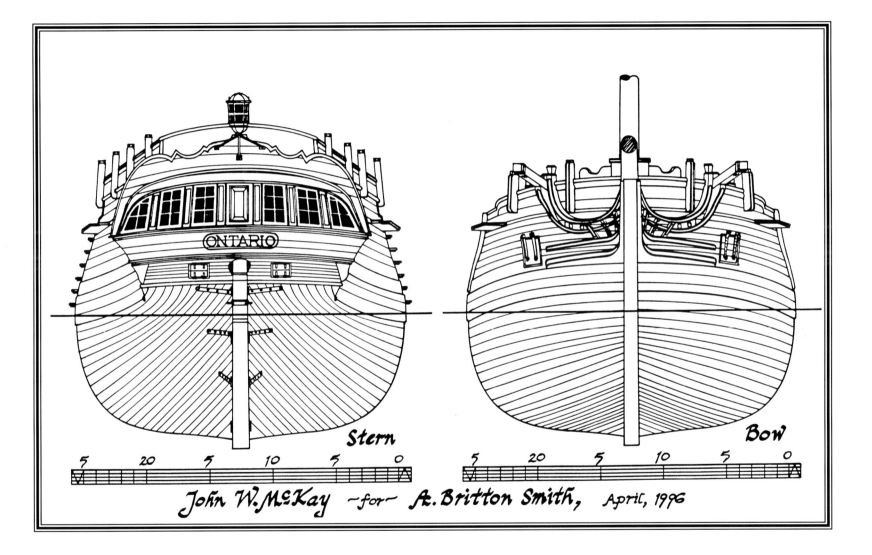

Stern

Bow

5   20   5   10   5   0

5   20   5   10   5   0

John W. McKay ~for~ A. Britton Smith,   April, 1996

Inboard Profile

Legend
H. M. Brig Sloop Ontario · Key list

1. Keel
2. Scarph
3. Frames
4. Keelson
5. Stem
6. Cutwater
7. Stern post
8. Rudder
9. Ante room
10. Passage
1.1. Fore peak (Magazine)
12. Fore Platform
13. [Possible powder stowage]
14. Hold
15. Well
16. Shot locker
17. Aft platform
18. Aft peak [Lady's hole]
19. Fore castle
20. Companionway
21. Waist
22. Gun port
23. Sweep port
24. Coach (Captain's dining room/office)
25. Great cabin
26. Head Rails
27. Bowsprit
28. Cat head
29. Fore mast
30. Fore castle deck
31. Windlass
32. Belfry
33. 20 foot Cutter
34. 16 foot Launch
35. Main mast
36. Trysail mast
37. Elm tree pump
38. Quarter deck
39. Swivel stantion
40. Binnacle
41. Tiller
42. Lantern

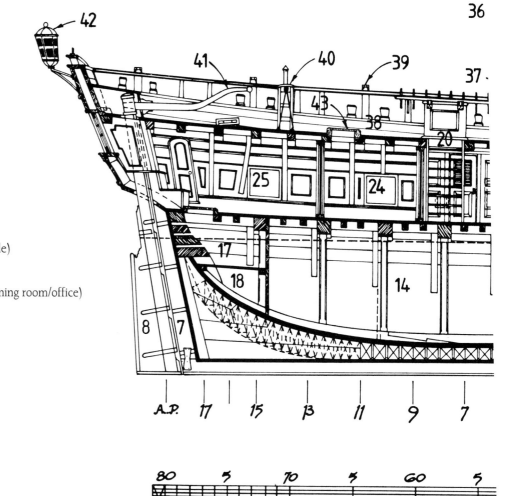

36

42 41 40 39 37

43 38 20

25 24

17

18

14

8 7

A.P. 17 15 13 11 9 7

80 5 70 5 60 5

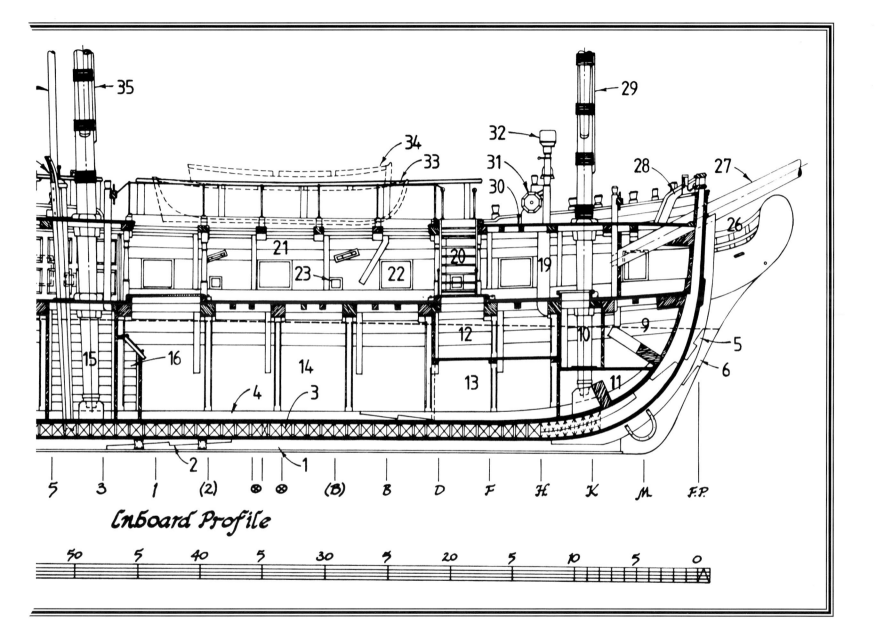

Inboard Profile

50 5 40 5 30 5 20 5 10 5 0

Upper Deck

Legend

1. Bowsprit
2. Head rails
3. Cat head
4. Swivel stantion
5. Bower anchor
6. Sheet anchor
7. Side ladder
8. Channel
9. Quarter Gallery
10. Bow chaser (6 pounder gun)
11. Fore mast
12. Belfry
13. Windlass
14. Forecastle deck
15. Companionway
16. 20 foot Cutter
17. 16 foot Launch
18. Waist
19. Main mast
20. Elm tree pump
21. Trysail mast
22. Booby hatch
23. Quarter deck
24. 4 pounder gun
25. Binnacle
26. Tiller
27. Stern chaser
   (4 pounder gun)
28. Shot garland
30. Skylight
29. Lantern

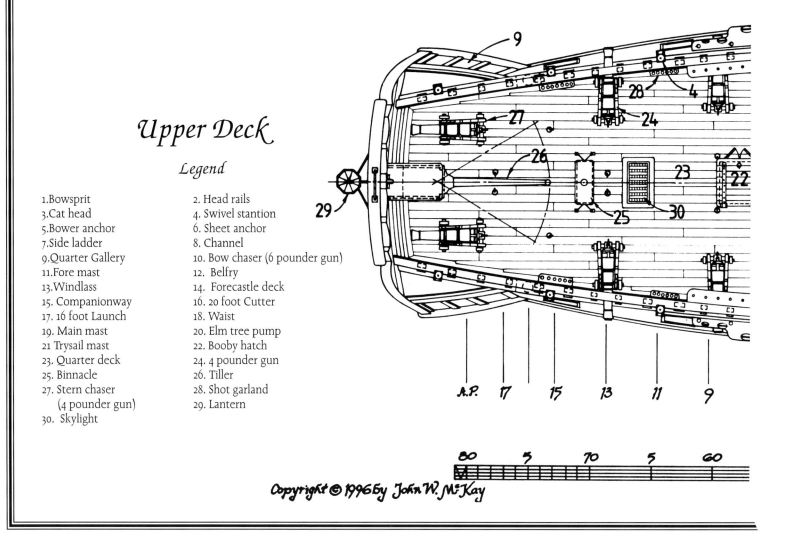

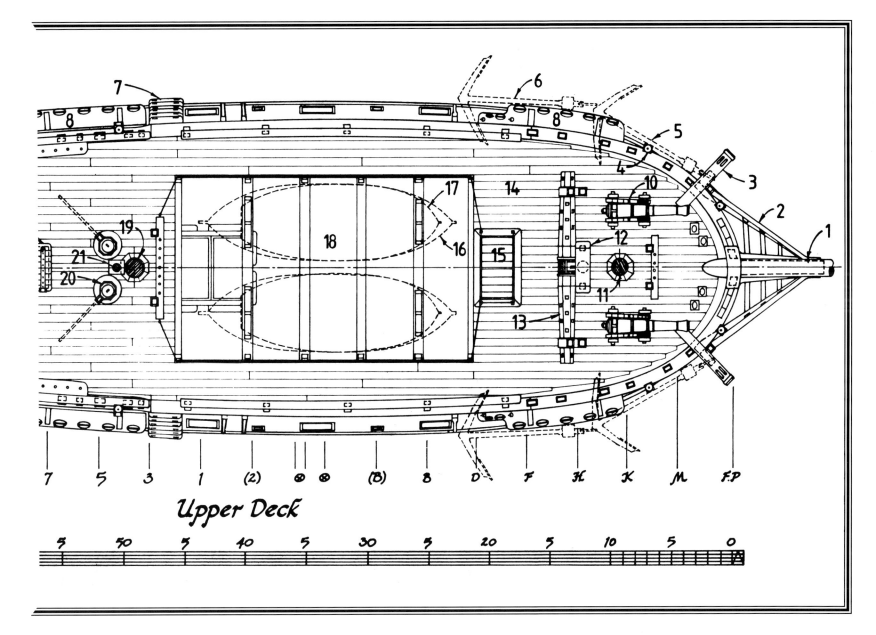

Upper Deck

Lower (Gun) Deck

Legend

1. Stem
2. Cutwater
3. Bowsprit
4. Foremast
5. Scuttle
6. Fore hatch
7. Ladder
8. Fore Castle
9. Grating
10. 6 pounder gun
11. Shot garland
12. Main mast
13. Elm tree pump
14. Main hatch
15. Starboard cabin [2 Officers]
16. Port cabin [2 Officers]
17. Side ladder
18. Coach
19. Captain's bed place
20. Great cabin
21. Stern post
22. Rudder
23. Quarter gallery
24. Canvas screen

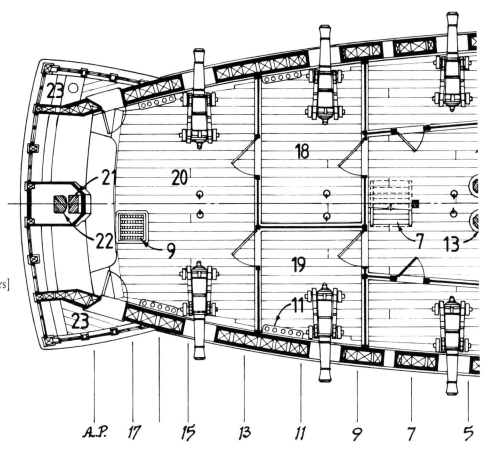

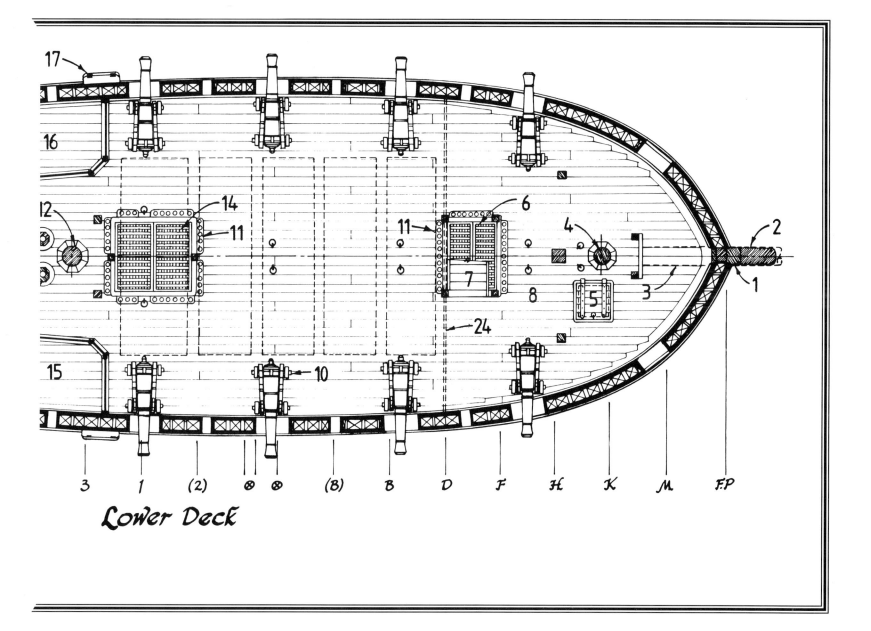

Lower Deck

Hold

Legend

1. Stem
2. Cutwater
3. Fore mast
4. Breast hook
5. Lantern
6. Filling room
7. Ante room
8. Passage
9. Scuttle (to magazine)
10. Fore platform
11. Hatch
12. Boatswain's store room
13. Carpenter's store room
14. Gunner's store room
15. Hold
16. Keelson
17. Pillar
18. Hanging knees
19. Main hatch over
20. Shot locker
21. Well
22. Main mast
23. Elm tree pump
24. [Possible powder stowage]
25. [Possible spirit room]
26. [Possible passenger accommodation]
27. Aft platform
28. Scuttle (to lady's hole)
29. Stern post
30. Rudder

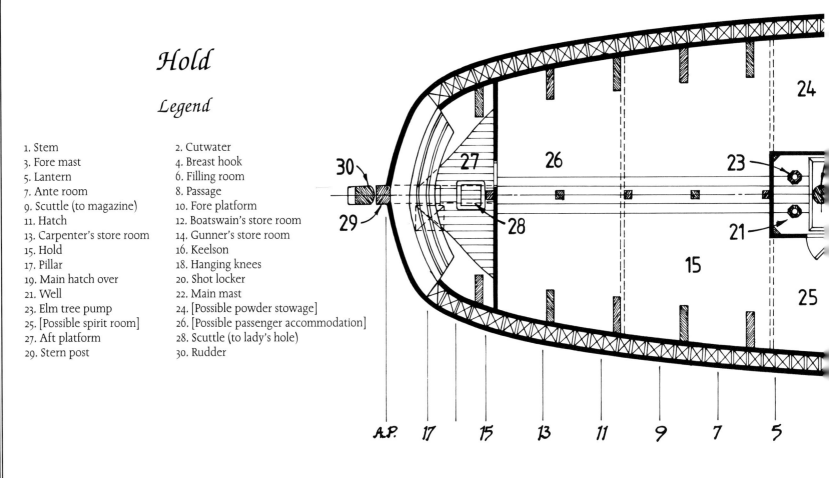

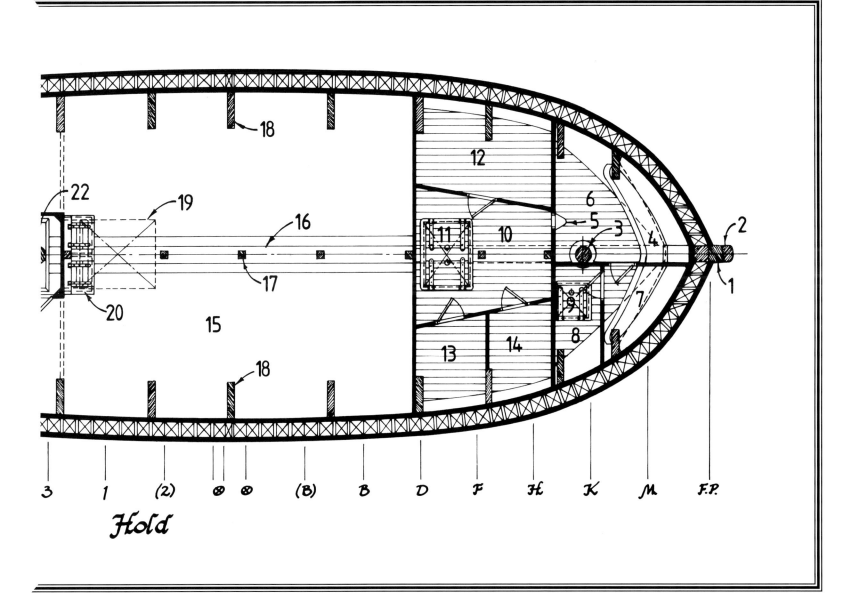

Hold

Cross Section at "B"
(Looking Forward) - Fore Mast

Legend

1. Keel
2. Frame
3. Keelson
4. Hold
5. Pillar
6. Hanging knee
7. Main deck
8. Gun port
9. Companionway
10. Hanging knee
11. Windlass
12. Belfry
13. Fore lower mast
14. Fore yard
15. Fore top mast
16. Fore topsail yard
17. Fore topgallant mast
18. Fore topgallant yard

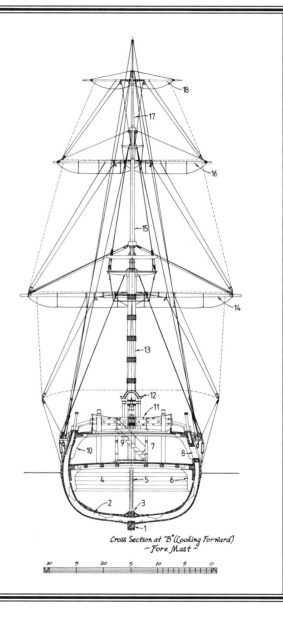

Cross Section at "B" (Looking Forward)
~ Fore Mast ~

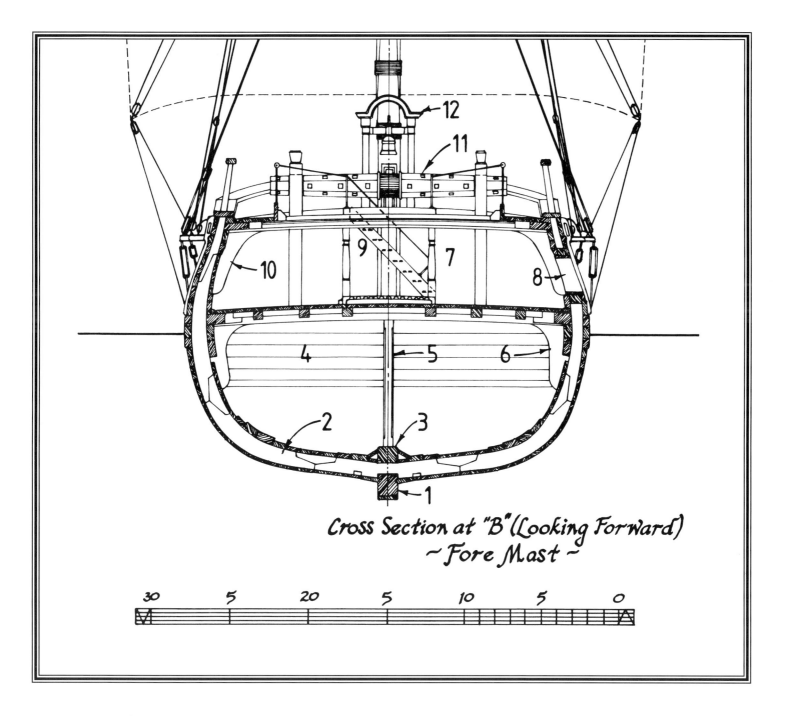

Cross Section at "B" (Looking Forward)
~ Fore Mast ~

30   5   20   5   10   5   0

Cross Section at "1"
(Looking Aft) - Main Mast

Legend

1. Keel
2. Frame
3. Keelson
4. Hold
5. Shot locker
6. Well
7. Hanging knee
8. Main deck
9. Main hatch
10. Gun port
11. Hanging knee
12. Waist
13. Elm tree pump
14. Main lower mast
15. Main yard
16. Main top mast
17. Main topsail yard
18. Main topgallant mast
19. Main topgallant yard

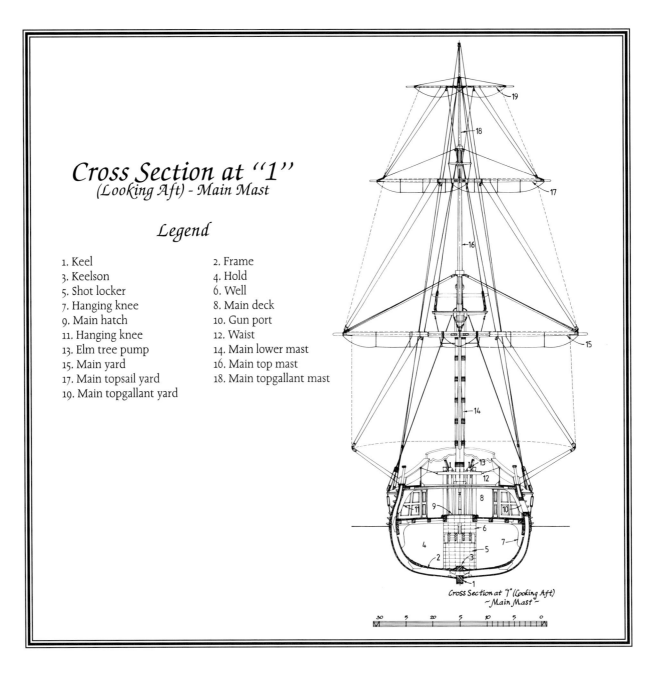

Cross Section at "1" (Looking Aft)
~Main Mast~

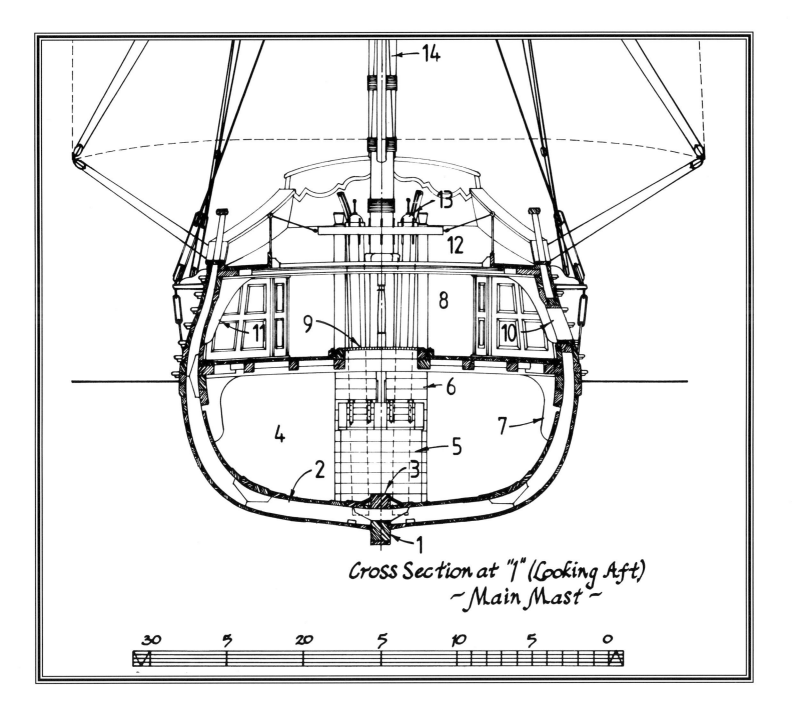

Cross Section at "1" (Looking Aft)
~ Main Mast ~

30   5   20   5   10   5   0

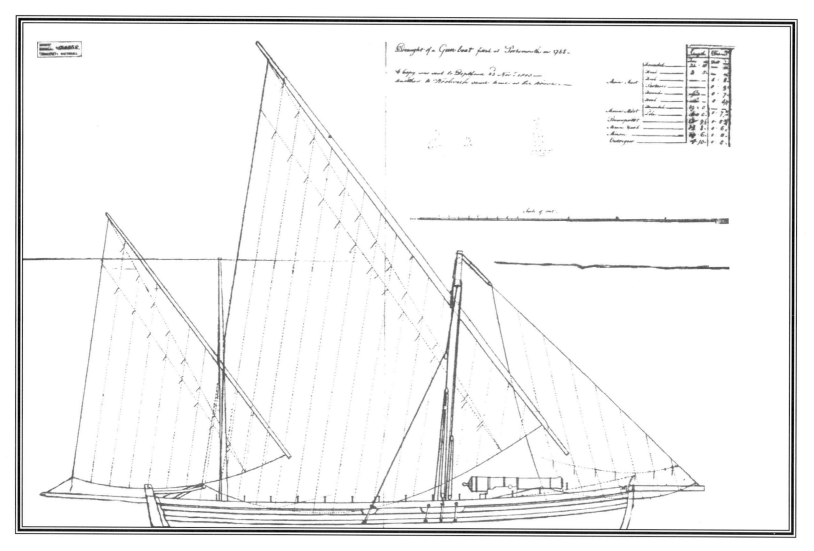

Admiralty draught of a 60-foot gun boat, 'as fitted'
lateen rig plan with one 18 pounder gun.

Launching Ontario

A letter from Robert Hamilton written in the spring of 1780 talks of the "new Vessel" and island life.

To Francis Goring, esq
Niagara

Carleton Island 25 March 1780

Dear Goring:

As I would not wish to pass an Opportunity of writing, I embrace this tho' it has no great Chance of reaching you before the Vessel. Shutt up from all Communication with the rest of the World, you cannot expect that this Barren Island will afford great Matter of Epistolary Entertainment. I have spent a very idle, tho' in other respects not a very uncomfortable Winter. Plenty to eat and Drink, and a good deal of other Amusements have made the Winter pass pretty pleasantly. With regard to my own motions if nothing extraordinary interfered I will not see my Niagara Friends 'till the second Trip of the Haldimand. At that time I hope to send up everything now under my Charge here. I will endeavor if possible to send our Wine by the first, that it may get on as fast as possible. On this however, I cannot promise, as there are 600 Barrels of Provisions and 100 men of the 34th to come up at that time.

Our new Vessel here will be launched as soon as the ice is gone and will be able to make a trip with the Haldimand when she returns from the first. She will be a noble Vessel for size as she will hold near a thousand Barrels. Make my comp's to Cunningham. As the Express is just going, I have not time to write him but will by the Vessel. Remember me also to _____ [torn out] with the same assurances to other inquiring Friends.

With sincerity Dear Goring, yours, & c.,
R. Hamilton

Two tumblers and a spoon made by François Ranvoyzé (1739-1819), silversmith of Quebec City. He served in Militia Company No. 5 during the siege by the Americans 1775-76.

By the end of March 1780 *Ontario's* hull was substantially complete and caulked. The iron chain-plates had been bolted on and the interior finishing and hardware was in place.

An elm timber launching cradle was assembled under the keel, resting on slipways that reached well out into the cove. Being still-green oak, they did not float, which was important. The rudder was hung, its four pintles resting in the four gudgeons, and the tiller lashed amidships to keep the launching straight (all ships, except Dutch, were launched stern first). Two bower anchors hung at the cat heads in case she broke free after her run to the river.

On May 10th the entire garrison assembled for the launch. About one thousand soldiers — from the 34th Regiment, the 47th Regiment, the 2nd battalion of the King's Royal Regiment of New York and the 2nd battalion of the 84th, The Royal Highland Emigrants — grasped the long cables stretching from the cradle and the brig along the shores of the cove. Seamen of the other vessels manned the two capstans on the beach. The carpenters waited by the chocks with sledge hammers, watching for the signal.

At the bow, on a decorated platform, stood John Coleman the builder, Captain James Andrews, Mrs. Elizabeth Andrews, down from Niagara, Captain John Schank, Mrs. Elizabeth Schank, Captain Alex Fraser of the 84th, commandant of the fort, Matriarch Molly Brant representing the Iroquois, Captain René La Force, and other commanders. The chaplain, Reverend John Bethune, said a short prayer. Captain Andrews uncorked a bottle of wine and poured it into tumblers for the guests. Elizabeth Andrews smashed the bottle, wrapped in ribbon, on an iron fishplate in the stem saying loudly, "I Christen thee *Ontario.*" Everyone cheered and raised their tumblers in a toast; the massed drums and fifes of all units burst forth loudly in "The White Cockade." The guns of the fort fired in salute as *Ontario* slowly slid, creaking and groaning, down the tallow-smeared ways, while the last chocks flew clear and the cables were strained by the muscular infantry.

With a roar, and a splash, the vessel entered the water. Her cradle was checked, and she floated free, gently rolling from side to side as if acknowledging the ringing cheers from the crowd. Then the official party moved to the now clear framing platform, where trestle tables were set in preparation for a light lunch, speeches, and many more toasts.

John Coleman, Master Shipwright, quietly slipped away to the yard office, now deserted. On his draughting table was the completed as-built drawing of the brig. He unstoppered his India ink bottle, chose a good quill pen, and wrote:

Reverend John Bethune (1750-1815), Chaplain of the 84th Foot, Royal Highland Emigrants, was the first Presbyterian clergyman in Upper Canada.

A draught of the Ontario, Launch'd at Carleton Island the 10 May 1780. Burthen in Tons 226 55/94.

P.S. Carleton Island is in Lake Ontario about 154 miles N.E. of Niagara

The tonnage noted by John Coleman on his draught was arrived at by the then current formula of: Length of keel x maximum beam x 1/2 maximum beam ÷ 94. He added a few measurements and signed his name, with three loops as a flourish, underneath. The drawing was then sealed in a copper tube addressed to "The Admiralty, Whitehall, London" and consigned to the mail bag. Although she was a Naval Department vessel, Mr. Coleman wanted to ensure that

A Draught of the Ontario Launch'd at Carleton Island the 10 May 1780
Length on the Lower Deck _____ 80..0
Of the Keel for Tonage _____ 64..0 ½
Breadth Extream _____ 25..0
Depth in Hold _____ 9..0
Burthen in Tons _____ 226 ½

P.S. Carleton Island is in Lake Ontario about 154 Miles N.E. of Niagara

C. Aldman

A List of Shipwrights engaged by Controller & Commissioner of the Naval Department and sent to Carleton Island

Names	Date of Engagement	When they left Quebec	
Joseph Recieux	1st Octor	15th Octor	
Francois Hannois	Do	Do	
Jos. Montmilleunt	Do	Do	Went from this to Montreal by Land with an Order of the Lieutenant Governors to the Captains of Militia to forward them with all expedition
Louis Marchand	Do	Do	
Jacques Compot	Do	Do	
André Tessier	Do	Do	
Franst. Lasseville	22d Octor	28th Octor	
Michel LaPort	Do	Do	
Jos. Carpentier	Do	Do	
Pre. Cholette	Do	Do	
Charle Bureau	Do	Do	Ditto — Ditto
Charle Rancin	Do	Do	
Charle Bernac	Do	Do	
Jean Fournel	Do	Do	
John Woolfenton	2d Novr	—	goes off 9th Novr by Water

N.B. Captain Schank Ordered the Master Builder to send one Foreman and four Shipwrights from Carleton Island to Detroit by a letter dated the 18th October

One Shipwright was always left at Niagara and upon Colonel Bolton's application I believe another was sent to that Post from Carleton Island _____

Quebec 8th Novemr 1779

Wm Robertson
L. Co. No. Dept

his achievement was permanently recorded. He then joined the group and poured a hefty rum for himself.

But for the seamen and artificers the rum ration had to wait. Within minutes *Ontario* was alongside the wharf, loading ballast. The gun carriages came next. Then the guns were slid in through the ports, hauled by their own tackles. On the other side of the cove her 53 foot pine mainmast already dangled from the towering sheer-legs set half way up the cliff, stayed by tackles from the ramparts.

Her armament consisted of six 4-pounder and sixteen 6-pounder guns. Two of these were ''long sixes'' mounted as bow-chasers on the fo'c'sle. The extra length gave this pair greater range. The other 6-pounders on the gun deck were shorter, their length limited by the space available for recoil and access to the muzzle for loading. The 4-pounders had more uncertain positioning. Four at least were probably on the quarterdeck as additional broad-side guns, and possibly two more faced astern on this level. Blind spots for most of the guns were directly astern and directly ahead, especially for a becalmed vessel. Therefore, one or two 4-pounders must have faced aft on the quarterdeck in normal circumstances. Her twelve swivel guns could be mounted in a variety of positions, even one or two in the tops, firing down. Pending action they were kept below, loaded but not primed. No carronades had been sent to Lake Ontario as yet. They were still a novelty in Canada.

A short 6-pounder gun, whose trunnions were knocked off at Fort Frontenac, now at Fort Henry, after retrieval from a hulk in Deadman Bay.

As far as possible, her cordage had been prepared in advance and labelled. Sails had been made in Quebec. Many tons of supplies of all sorts, blocks, and iron work had come up by bateau from Montreal, load after load, dragged along the shallows around the rapids by teams of toiling boatmen, aided at a few places by hired horses or oxen. Only ''The Cascades'' canal was in use, and it was little more than a ditch, hastily dug in 1779 with three short sections opened that

Stern Lantern.
Drawing by
John W. McKay.

fall. Lieut. William Twiss and his engineers get credit for the speedy completion. It only had two locks, but cut out the worst of the lower rapids and greatly expedited the shipment of heavy cargoes such as anchors and guns.

Ontario had a fairly ornate counter, with a scalloped taffrail, massive stern lantern, and rising from the rail, a vertical jackstaff from which fluttered a Red Ensign 16 feet long. A huge Union Jack was also hoisted temporarily at the bow for the launch. She had no figure head, but instead a simple curled beak beneath her bowsprit. Below the waterline she was tarred pitch-black and above painted yellow ochre. These were standard colours for King's ships at the time, as several water-colour paintings of the 1780s attest, and of which one, painted at Niagara, shows the Lake Ontario squadron at anchor.

On May 9th, 1780 Captain René LaForce was appointed superintendent of the civil department of the dockyard at Carleton, enabling John Coleman to take a well-earned leave. It may well be that language problems had arisen because few of the Quebec shipwrights spoke fluent English, as a list of the shipwrights sent to Carleton Island in October 1779 to work on *Ontario* suggests. John Woolfenton is the sole English surname on the list. It is unlikely that Mr. Coleman spoke much Canadian French. Captain LaForce was bilingual and had been involved in ship construction since the days of the French yard at Cataraqui. John Coleman was sent back to Carleton in November to supervise the building of *Limnade*, because LaForce had "gone down to Canada" after a dispute with Captain Bouchette. This arose over the succession to Captain Andrews as Commodore of Lake Ontario. Each felt entitled to the promotion.

At any rate, credit for the speedy construction of *Ontario*, on an island remote from all sources of supply and labour, belongs to Mr. John Coleman and Captain John Schank. She began her short career on her namesake lake in the summer of 1780.

Previous Page: *A bateau in the first stone lock on the St. Lawrence River, 1781. Note the deck cleats for the pole-pushers. From a lithograph by Rex Woods.*

Opposite: Seneca, Ontario, *and* Haldimand *at the Carleton Island anchorage in May 1780.* Ontario *is setting sail for Niagara on a south wind and has just fired a morning salute from her starboard-bow 6-pounder. Painting by Peter Rindlisbacher.*

Ruins of Fort Haldimand c. 1850.

Shipyard at Point Frederick, Kingston, c. 1792.

Fort Niagara from the Canadian shore, c. 1784, with Caldwell portrayed left and an unidentified topsail schooner centre.

Niagara River with Navy Hall (right), c. 1792.
From a painting by Mrs Elizabeth Posthuma Simcoe.

Left: Naval Lieutenant.
Right: Master and Commander of a brig-sloop.
Paintings by Dominic Serres, 1777.

Below: A Sea-service flint lock pistol.
Note belt-hook on left side.

Left: Private of the 78th Foot
(Fraser's Highlanders) c. 1762.

Right: Field Officer of the 84th Foot
(Royal Highland Emigrants), c. 1778.
Paintings by Robert J. Marrion for the
Canadian War Museum.

The SOUTH VIEW of OSWEGO on LAKE ONTARIO

General Shirley in 1755 Strengthen'd & inlarged, this Fort and erected two others; one Westward 170 Square with a Rampart of Earth & Stone. Another on the Opposite side of the Bason, 470 Yards distant from the Old Fort. This which is call'd the East Fort, is built of Logs and

the Wall is surrounded by a Ditch. The Projection of the Rocks, renders the Channel at the Entrance into the Onondaga River very Narrow, and our Vessels are generally warp'd from the Lake into the Bason.

Copied by D Vaughan from Smiths Hist. N.Y. Qto. Lond. 1757

Engraved & Printed by Gentil B

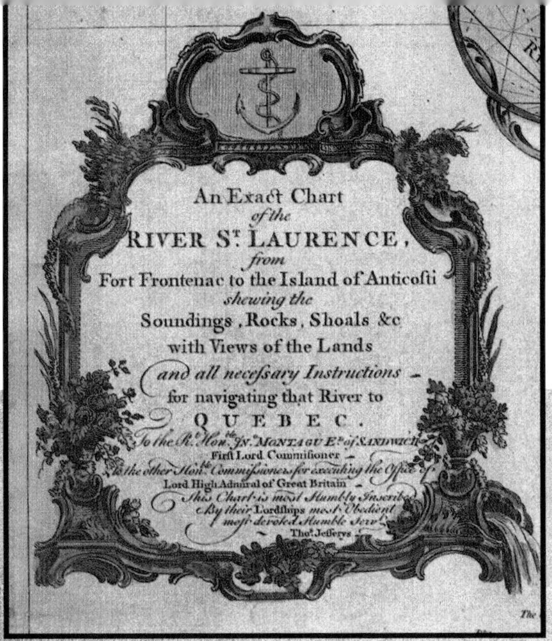

An Exact Chart
of the
RIVER St. LAURENCE,
from
Fort Frontenac to the Island of Anticosti
shewing the
Soundings, Rocks, Shoals &c
with Views of the Lands
and all necessary Instructions
for navigating that River to
QUEBEC.

To the Rt. Honble. Js. MONTAGU Eal. of SANDWICH
First Lord Commissioner
& to the other Honble. Commissioners for executing the Office of
Lord High Admiral of Great Britain
This Chart is most Humbly Inscribed
By their Lordships most Obedient
most devoted Humble Servt.
Thos. Jefferys

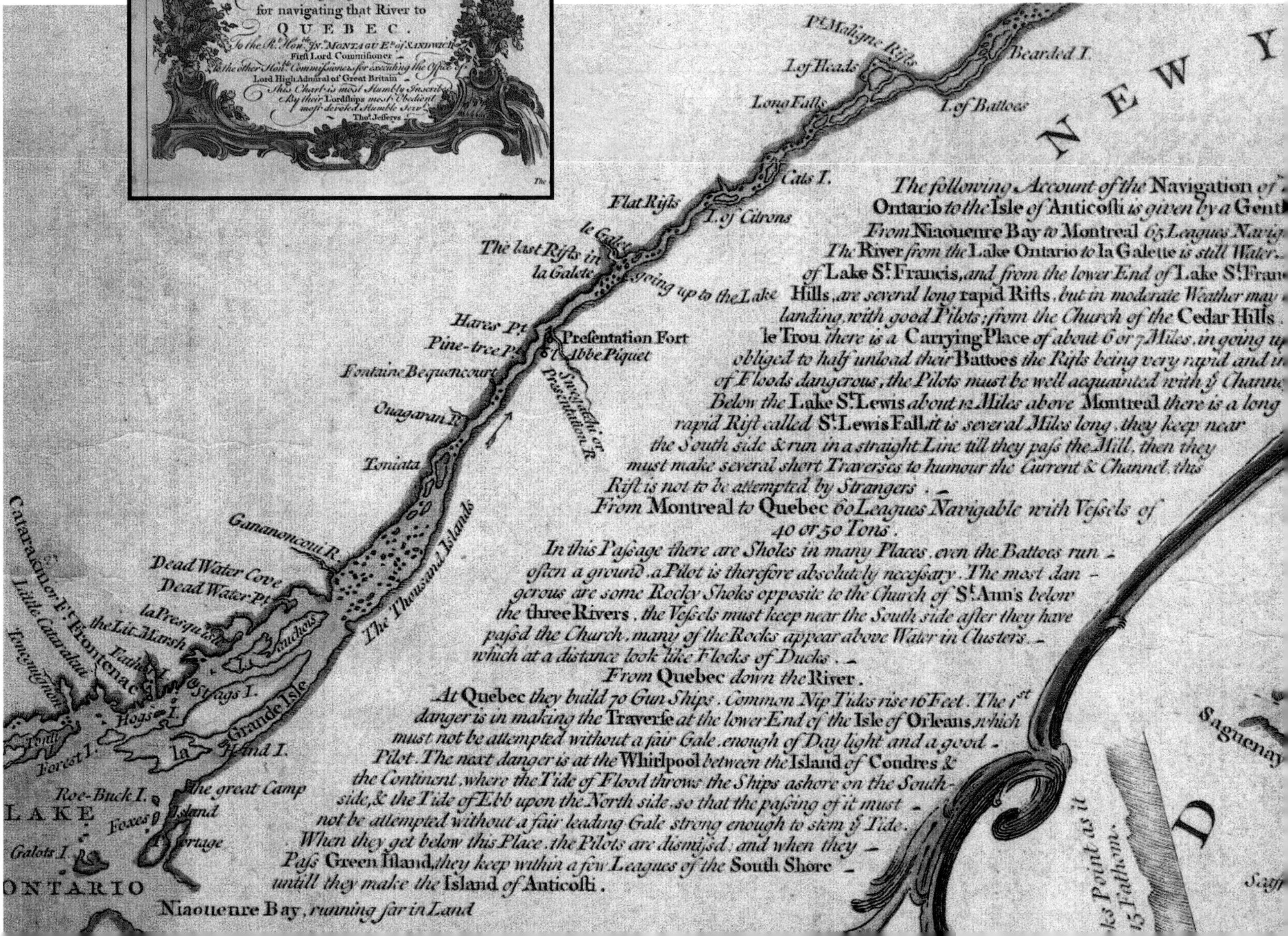

NEW Y[ORK]

Pt. Maligne Rifts
Bearded I.
I. of Heads
Long Falls
I. of Battoes

Cats I.
Flat Rifts
le Galet
I. of Citrons
The last Rifts in
la Galete   going up to the Lake

Hares Pt.
Pine-tree Pt.   Presentation Fort
Fontaine Bequencourt   l'Abbe Piquet
Swegatchi or Presentation R.
Ouagaran R.

Toniata

Gananoncoui R.

Dead Water Cove
Dead Water Pt.
la Presqu'isle
the Lit. Marsh
Cataraqui or Ft. Frontenac
Tenewegnon
la Petite Cataraqui
Faucheis
Stags I.
Hogs I.
Trout I.
Forest I.   la Wind I.
Grande Isle
The Thousand Islands

Roe-Buck I.
Foxes I.
the great Camp Island
Galots I.
Portage

LAKE

ONTARIO

Niaouenre Bay, running far in Land

The following Account of the Navigation of
Ontario to the Isle of Anticosti is given by a Gentl.
From Niaouenre Bay to Montreal 65 Leagues Navig.
The River from the Lake Ontario to la Galette is still Water
of Lake St. Francis, and from the lower End of Lake St. Fran
Hills, are several long rapid Rifts, but in moderate Weather may
landing, with good Pilots; from the Church of the Cedar Hills
le Trou there is a Carrying Place of about 6 or 7 Miles, in going up
obliged to half unload their Battoes the Rifts being very rapid and in
of Floods dangerous, the Pilots must be well acquainted with ye Channe
Below the Lake St. Lewis about 12 Miles above Montreal there is a long
rapid Rift called St. Lewis Fall, it is several Miles long, they keep near
the South side & run in a straight Line till they pass the Mill, then they
must make several short Traverses to humour the Current & Channel, this
Rift is not to be attempted by Strangers.
From Montreal to Quebec 60 Leagues Navigable with Vessels of
40 or 50 Tons.
In this Passage there are Sholes in many Places, even the Battoes run
often a ground, a Pilot is therefore absolutely necessary. The most dangerous are some Rocky Sholes opposite to the Church of St. Ann's below
the three Rivers, the Vessels must keep near the South side after they have
passed the Church, many of the Rocks appear above Water in Clusters
which at a distance look like Flocks of Ducks.
From Quebec down the River.
At Quebec they build 70 Gun Ships. Common Nip Tides rise 16 Feet. The 1st
danger is in making the Traverse at the lower End of the Isle of Orleans, which
must not be attempted without a fair Gale, enough of Day light and a good
Pilot. The next danger is at the Whirlpool between the Island of Coudres &
the Continent, where the Tide of Flood throws the Ships ashore on the South
side, & the Tide of Ebb upon the North side, so that the passing of it must
not be attempted without a fair leading Gale strong enough to stem ye Tide.
When they get below this Place, the Pilots are dismiss'd, and when they
Pass Green Island, they keep within a few Leagues of the South Shore
untill they make the Island of Anticosti.

Saguenay

Pt. as it
15 Fathom.
Sag

D

A view of Cataraqui from Capt. Joseph Brant's house on the Cataraqui
River, July 1784, showing Seneca docked and Limnade arriving.
A detail from a painting by James Peachey.

A view of Cataraqui on Lake Ontario,
August 1783, with Limnade docked (right).
From a painting by James Peachey.

Limnade *(left)* and Seneca *(right)* off Wolfe Island.
Painting by Peter Rindlisbacher.

Captain John Schank

Captain James Andrews

Colonel John Butler

Ontario At Work

A considerable back-log of freight for Niagara, Detroit, and the other western posts had accumulated in the merchant's warehouses despite early trips by *Seneca*, *Mohawk*, *Caldwell*, and *Haldimand*, the other Naval Department vessels on the lake. A substantial pay-load was taken aboard for the maiden voyage of *Ontario* to Niagara. Earlier, a quick one day shake-down cruise had been used to adjust ballast for proper trim, tighten standing rigging, and test stability with lee guns run out one-by-one, close-hauled in a fresh breeze. This was a nerve-wracking procedure, but very important reassurance of her sea-worthiness.

Throughout the summer of 1780 *Ontario* transported troops, stores, and civilian merchandise around and across Lake Ontario, stopping at Niagara and Carleton Island frequently, down the river to Oswegatchie occasionally, and making regular checks at Oswego.

Lengthy calm periods caused delay in August, resulting in Robert Macaulay, one of the merchants on Carleton Island, sending two letters to Francis Goring by the same trip of *Ontario*.

Carleton Island 25 Aug't 1780

Dear Goring

    I have wrote to you A few Days pas'ed wich you have not received as yett as the Ontario has not any wind to carry her out of the Harber as yett. I have taken this Second Thought about the Stove, I find it is not save _____ as I thought at first and as there was other people wanting of hitt I now Sent it by the Ontario, and please Consider Mr. Archd. Thomson for the Same as the Stove be loungs to his Dedy in house — Mackay —

    In Closed you will find your own Acc't, and After you Examine it pray Lett me know if there is any thing a miss as Mr. Gray is not heer. I am not positive whether he his Sett down every-thing wright or not as to Mr. Robinson the Preacher (?) you must Receive his Acc't be fore you pay it.

    Not any Nuse from Montreal this Loung Time. I am much Afraid we will have a bad acc't of the fleet. How Ever keep that to your Self — and belive me to be your very

Humble Servant
Robt. Macaulay

Mr. Francis Goring

Buttons of the 21st (Royal North British Fusiliers) and the 53rd (King's Shropshire Light Infantry).

A steady trickle of Loyalists rested a few days at Fort Ontario after the arduous journey up the Mohawk, before rowing on along the lake shore to Niagara and Burlington Bay. Frequently these people needed help in the form of food, boat repairs, and advice. Many had relatives serving in Butler's Rangers, the KRR of New York, or the Royal Highland Emigrants, all units then stationed around the lake. Free passage was granted to desperate cases, others could pay. Most of those with money headed down river for Quebec and Montreal — at least the women and children did. The fit men usually enlisted in one of the units in garrison at Fort Haldimand or Fort Niagara.

That year, 1780, Macaulay built a log house outside the fort, which he had rafted to Cataraqui after the war, one of three moved in 1783. Clapboarded, it stood on the corner of Princess and Ontario Streets until demolished in 1928.

Over the years many eighteenth-century artifacts have been found in gardens and excavations on Carleton Island, including such civilian articles as shoe buckles, ornate coat-buttons and parts of non-military weapons. This would indicate that a considerable number of Loyalists passed through the Carleton Island refugee camp. As well, uniform buttons of several British regiments have turned up. Not only of the KRRNY, Butler's Rangers, the 8th, 34th, 47th and 84th which are to be expected, but also those of other units not known to have been in garrison. Possibly these are from prisoners of the Rebels, exchanged at Fort Stanwyx and re-mustered in new units with different regimental insignia. Buttons of the 21st (Royal North British Fusiliers) and the 53rd (King's Shropshire Light Infantry) support this theory, as both these battalions were interned by the Americans at Saratoga in 1777.

Life aboard this working ship was cramped. The upper deck was a bit cluttered of necessity. Just inside the taffrail, two 4-pounder guns sat, one on each side of the rudder post, pointed aft. Ahead of them the tiller required a free arc. The box binnacle stood just next, flanked by two more 4-pounder guns on each side, then the removable glass skylight or companion serving the captain's quarters below. Four swivel guns were mounted on the sturdy gunwale. A ladderway, covered by the booby hatch, led down to the officer's cabins. Next to the 18 inch mainmast were the two bilge pumps, with long removable handles enabling several men to pump at a shift. Around both masts were pinrails for belaying pins. Just forward of the quarterdeck was the open waist, covered, usually, with cedar and walnut gratings except for a ladder space. Two more swivel guns were mounted here on stanchions.

Macaulay House, originally a log house outside the fort, then rafted to Cataraqui (Kingston) after the war, one of three moved in 1783. Clapboarded, it stood on the corner of Princess and Ontario Streets until demolished in 1928.

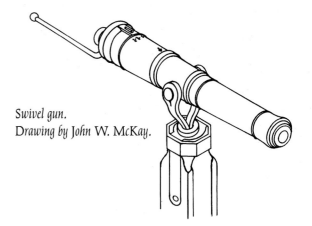

Swivel gun. Drawing by John W. McKay.

Amidships on the beams sat two whale-boats, needed for towing in flat calm or emergency, and nested in them, two cutters for messages and visits ashore. Also located here were two more swivel stanchions and several spare spars. The windlass, with room to work, was on the fo'c's'le. Above it hung the brass bell in a carved frame or belfry. To the side, the galley stove-pipe stuck up. Then came the foremast, 16 inches in diameter, mooring bitts and cathead each side, bower and best bower anchors lashed outboard, stream and sheet anchors secured behind them. A pair of 6-pounders, called bow-chasers, faced forward. Then under the bowsprit, the open, drafty head, one rail to sit on, one to lean on and one to rest the feet.

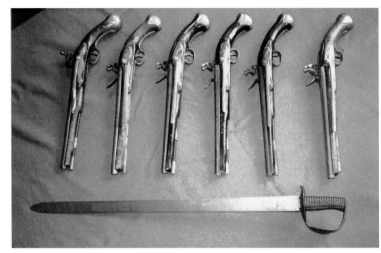

Three pairs of long sea-service pistols, all with belt hook, and a cutlass, usable either left or right-handed.

Below, when cleared for action and bulkheads stowed, the gun deck was wide open for all 80 feet of its length. In normal use, light, easily removable partitions, mostly canvas, gave each officer a private cabin, shared with a gun, all under the quarterdeck.

Forward of the main hatch was the home of the forty seamen and fifty soldier-marines who made up the crew. Over each gun was a hanging mess table surrounded by the men's chests. Upon these they sat to eat, play cards, make clothes, read or write letters, usually by the light of hanging lanterns. Each deck beam had an oak tie rail fastened to it from which were hung the hammocks of those crewmen off watch. Also secured to the beams were cutlasses, pikes, and the various rammers, sponges, worms, and handspikes required for the guns.

Very little space was wasted. Passenger's hammocks were slung in the hold, over the cargo. A hammock was made of heavy canvas, 6 feet long and 3 feet wide, with grommets and cords at each end. A thin mattress, 5 feet 10 inches by 2 feet 3 inches and a small pillow were issued to each man. These were both stuffed with oakum or rope-yarn — old worn-out rope picked apart by crew members undergoing punishment. Much oakum was also required to caulk the seams of new vessels built at the shipyard and to make wads for guns. The sailor defaulters produced more than enough!

For the usual number of women and children carried, the aftmost part of the hold was partitioned off and rigged with fixed berths. In vessels steered by a wheel, the tiller projected from the rudder post just below the gun deck beams. Rope tackles leading down from the quarterdeck controlled its movement. This steering gear reduced the headroom here, and the squealing blocks let everyone know of a course change. The steerage consequently became the cheapest accommodation for sea travellers. Water buckets and chamber pots were the only amenities provided, but the voyage usually lasted only a few days, even if from Niagara to Oswegatchie. Opening the stern gunports allowed some light and air into the steerage area, when conditions permitted. Many of the crew and some passengers slept on deck in good weather. Particularly on hot summer nights, the open air was much preferred.

A seaman's chest. The rope handles were often hardened with tar.

Two transverse bulkheads about 7 feet apart divided the hold at the mainmast. The port side compartment was the powder magazine, with all its safety features and rules. Here the gunpowder for the *Ontario* herself was carried and, as well, any being shipped for merchants or to supply garrisons to the west. On the starboard side was a large locker for valuable merchandise such as trade-silver, rum, brandy, tea, tobacco, and firearms. Between the two was the pump well. Barrels, boxes, and bales were stowed in the main hold amidships.

Long planks and boards were passed in through the stern gunports and carried forward past the pump shafts and mainmast. The triangular space under the aft platform, accessible through a hatch, was called the Lady's Hole because the Gunner, in times past, was nick-named "The Lady," and this peak was reserved for his stores. Shot could be transferred back here to correct trim. It also did duty as the captain's wine cellar, there being a convenient hatch leading directly upward to the great cabin from the platform. A pair of swivel guns firing through the transom ports would defend against boat-borne attacks from astern.

Ontario, although a "King's Ship," was a vessel of the Naval Department, later called the Provincial Marine, a separate Canadian naval force operating on the lakes, and administered by the Quartermaster General of the Army in Canada from 1765 until 1813. Of necessity it borrowed a few officers and much material from the Royal Navy. It consisted, in 1780, of small squadrons on Lakes Champlain, Ontario, Erie, and a couple of schooners plying Lake Huron. It also operated shipyards at locations on each lake. Most of its officers were Canadians and had been civilian skippers of small lake trading schooners in peace time. A couple of the older ones had served in the French barques until 1760; Captain LaForce, for example, had commanded the French *Iroquoise* and Captain LaBroquerie *Outaoaise* in the battle of the St. Lawrence.

The seamen were a very mixed lot, sailing in the April to November season, and trapping, logging, or working in the shipyards in winter. Many were youths looking for adventure or for an escape from the family farm. Others were career professionals with a dislike for months-long ocean voyages and the strict discipline of deep-water service. Combined, these men developed a strong esprit-de-corps and great pride in their "boats" (for some reason every vessel built for fresh water was, and is, called a "boat," rather than a ship). As it was wartime, they adopted a voluntary shore uniform of short blue jacket, white duck trousers, tarred straw hat, black pumps with large shoe buckles, and black neckerchief. White shirts were army issue. Their jacket buttons

"Anchor" button found on Carleton Island.

were the very large, round ones of the time, bearing a beaver and the word "Canada." These were cast from pewter or lead and enamelled yellow. Some have been found on Carleton Island bearing only an anchor design, probably from Royal Navy personnel. This "salty" uniform, called "Tiddley Clothes," gave them a sense of identity when drinking in the sutlers' taverns with members of Butler's Rangers or the various line regiments, all of whom boasted regimental brass buttons and unit belt plates. Lieutenant Peachey painted some Provincial Marine "bluejackets" ashore at Cataraqui in 1783, chatting up local belles.

The seaman's personal weapons were the long sea-service flintlock pistol and the cutlass. The pistol was 19 inches long overall with a 12 inch steel barrel, walnut stock and brass fittings. On the left side it had a long steel belt hook so that it could be carried hands-free for boarding an enemy. The cutlass was about 33 inches long with a 1 1/2 wide flat blade.

Ontario's commander and also commodore of the lake squadron was Captain James Andrews. A native of Scotland, he was both experienced and well-trained professionally. Andrews had been captain of the schooner *Dunmore* on Lake Erie before his promotion to Commodore in *Haldimand*. His wife Elizabeth and their son and two daughters lived at or near Navy Hall in what is now Niagara-on-the-Lake. The lieutenant was a Mr. Plau, not yet further identified. His name is not found in the various lists of commissions and appointments in the Haldimand Papers. Neither Mr. Plau nor Captain James Andrews appear in indexes of Royal Navy lieutenants for 1780 or prior years.

Besides these two commissioned officers and about forty seamen of the Provincial Marine, the crew numbered several petty officers. These included the first mate, the bo'sun, the carpenter, and the gunner. Their rank entitled them to a small cabin each, on the platform in the fore part of the hold. The position of gunner may have been filled by one of the artillerymen on board,

A Naval Department button. Drawn by Ted Zuber from an eighteenth-century author's description.

as responsibility for the powder magazine demands training in the care and preparation of explosives.

The rank of midshipman does not appear to have been in use. However, in 1779 General Haldimand appointed seven young gentlemen to be "Volunteers on the Lakes." One, Adam McAllan, was named volunteer in April, then in October commissioned as "Lieutenant on the Lakes." This seems to be a very short cadetship, but he had served as first mate of *Haldimand* for the previous two years. *Ontario* probably had two or three of these officers-in-training included in the number of her seamen.

All of the vessels carried, in addition, a complement of soldiers serving as marines. In action, these did duty as marksmen, manned the swivel guns and filled out the gun crews, leaving most of the sailors free to work the ship. In 1780 it was the turn of the 34th Foot, The Cumberland Regiment, to supply the marine detachments for Lake Ontario, with the balance of the battalion stationed in garrison at Carleton Island. A brig or snow normally carried one or two infantry officers, two sergeants, one drummer, fifty to sixty men, and four or five soldier's wives. The wives drew rations but no pay. They did much of the cooking, laundry, and uniform repairs.

In 1780 the daily ration for seamen and artificers at the Upper Posts of Carleton, Niagara, and Detroit was 1 1/2 pounds flour or biscuit, 1 pound beef or 8 ounces pork, 1/4 pint pease, 1 ounce butter, 1 ounce oatmeal or rice — total value two York Shillings. The oatmeal was usually served as a thin gruel called "skilly." The dried peas were boiled with pork bones to make pea soup. Fish caught over the side was a popular meal, and could also be bartered in port for fresh vegetables or eggs. An ordinary seaman's pay was six pence a day. A half-gill rum ration was issued in cases of severe hardship or exhausting work, but not as a regular item.

Aboard ship the soldiers went barefoot in summer, wore issue canvas fatigue trousers and white issue shirts. The red tunics and white crossbelts still

A *seaman of* Ontario *dressed up to go ashore. Sketch by Ted Zuber.*

came out occasionally, however, when a salute was called for. Entering or leaving harbour, welcoming an important person aboard or passing another large vessel within hailing distance, meant a parade on the quarter-deck, "Present Arms," drum roll, and slap-slap of muskets.

For woodland service, the army units on the Great Lakes were given permission to de-brim their hats, just leaving a peak over the eyes, cut short their tunics a little below the waist, and dull the bright red to a rust shade. For fighting and patrolling in the bush, the parade ground uniform had proven to be a suicidal handicap far too many times. Haversacks and knapsacks were blackened with shoe blacking. White cross belts were left in barrack boxes. White breeches were replaced by Iroquois-made fringed doeskin leggings. Moosehide moccasins became the issue footwear. Each man carried a steel tomahawk and sheath knife in addition to his bayonet. Much of this change was copied from the Rangers who went a step further and adopted green tunics, later to be a prerogative of the rifle corps.

They rowed the ship's boats when towing was necessary (along with their sailor friends), heaved on a line or the windlass, stood watch, cleaned ship, stowed cargo, and generally helped in everything except handling sail aloft. "No soldiers higher than the tops" was the order, tops being the large platforms on each mast easily reached via the shrouds. Army pay, though low (eight pence per day), was slightly better than the Provincial Marine, which led to many letters of complaint from sailors, addressed to General Haldimand, on the subject of money.

The drummer, who was often an under-age soldier, acted as messenger and beat various signals on his drum when ordered to do so. This rarely happened, but when the sweeps were out to row the vessel into a narrow harbour such as Oswego, or to aid the boats in towing against the river current, he came into his own. Beating time for the "galley slaves," as the soldiers called themselves, was essential to co-ordinate the efforts of those handling the long,

A *private of the 34th Foot dressed for woodland service. Sketch by Ted Zuber.*

awkward, two-man oars. A long drum roll and a sharp thump marked each stroke. While the Admiralty draught for *Ontario* does not show sweep-ports, sweeps were standard equipment for vessels up to about 300 tons. They could be used on the upper deck between pairs of bitts, as well.

A major concern of Captain Andrews was the ever-present danger of an attempt by the Americans to seize one or more of the large armed vessels. To defeat them in battle would require taking a large gunboat force down the Onondaga River to Lake Ontario. A very difficult portage at Oswego Falls (now Fulton, New York) meant that the size of such boats was limited, and the gun in each would therefore be too small to outrange those of the British vessels. Further, Onondaga scouts would take word to Carleton Island of any American expedition moving toward the lake, so that the whole British flotilla would be assembled off Oswego waiting to greet them with loaded cannon.

The alternative was to capture *Ontario*, the most powerful vessel on the lake. To this end, hostile Oneida patrols watched the narrow channels of the Thousand Islands and shadowed the vessel between Oswegatchie and Carleton. On each trip down river it was necessary to anchor for the night at least once, usually on the westbound leg. This was the most vulnerable area, as canoes could sneak up close behind the islands permitting Oneidas and American soldiers to swarm aboard without warning.

To counter this threat, the crew of *Ontario* was kept strong in numbers. The swivel guns were loaded with a half-pound bag of buckshot and mounted on the rails when in the river. Half the crew were on watch under arms when anchored, and every effort was made to have several vessels travel in convoy for mutual defence, not only in the St. Lawrence but also on the lake. A becalmed vessel close to shore could be attacked by canoe anywhere, anytime, but the greatest danger was at night.

Had the Americans and their Oneida allies been able to board *Ontario*

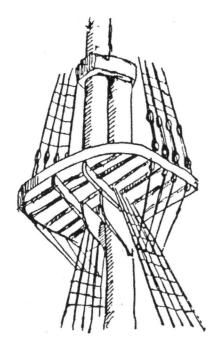

The Maintop.

some moonlight night and take her, then with her guns they could in turn have sunk or captured *Seneca*, *Haldimand*, and the smaller boats with ease. With command of the lake, the two-thousand-man garrison of Northern New York would be in a position to besiege Fort Haldimand, then, once it fell, to advance down-river upon Montreal and Quebec.

This fear of surprise attack and boarding was behind the uncomfortably large number of soldiers usually carried. It also meant many hours of weapons training for the crew. Empty bottles were used as targets for pistol shooting. Canvas dummies were hacked and stabbed. Cutlass drill and bayonet practice built up the muscles of the sailors and soldiers.

Perhaps because of the defensive strength of the vessels, no actual assault on them is recorded, although Carleton Island workers were taken prisoner from time to time, even in broad daylight, by daring American patrols. On at least one occasion, General Haldimand was worried to the point of ordering despatches for Colonel Bolton to be encased in lead. Lieutenant Tyce was told to throw them overboard should the Americans intercept him. The General's concern is also expressed in this letter to Col. Bolton, commandant at Niagara.

Blockhouse built on the point at Carleton Island in 1779. From J.H. Durham.

To Col. Bolton

Quebec the 31st July, 1778

Sir,

* * * * * I would observe to you the necessity of your being very particular in respect of the precautions necessary to be observed upon all occasions On board the Armed Vessels against the attempts of the Rebels upon them by Boats and other Stratagems for which purpose they should at no time allow even a Canoe or Boat of any kind to board them till they are well assured of them being Friends, nor ever bring the Vessels to anchor in their Passages or Cruises, so near the Land

A 'Lanthorne'.

*as to be liable to be fired upon or Surprised: and every endeavour must be exerted to excite in the Officers Serving in that Employ, a spirit of the utmost Vigilance and Activity. * * * * **

I am Sir
Fred'k Haldimand

As a further precaution, recognition signals for vessels were laid down, as follows:

By Day — The Ship to Windward shall Hoist an English Jack at the Fore Top Gallant Mast Head which the Ship to Leeward is to answer by Hoisting a Red Ensign at the Main Top Gallant Mast Head. Then the Ship to Windward shall take in the English Jack from the Fore Top Gallant Mast Head and Hoist a French Jack in its Stead and Fire one Gunn. The Ship to Leeward shall then Hoist a Blue Ensign at the Fore Top Gallant Mast Head without taking in the Red Ensign at the Main Top Gallant Mast Head.

These Signals will be made at the Head of Top Mast or Lower Masts in Vessels not having Top Gallant Masts up, and the Signals Ordered to be made at the Main Top Gallant Mast Head of Vessels of three or two Masts is to be made by Sloops at the Gaff end.

By Night — The Ship to Windward shall show three Lights at equal Distance a Breast of each other and the Ship to Leeward shall answer by showing four Lights at equal Distance one above the other, then Boath Ships shall take in their Lights and show two of equal Height a Breast keeping them up, until they have Hailed each other.

In a Fogg — In case of hearing Gunns Fired in a Fogg, Bells Ringing or Drums Beating the Ship that makes such Discovery shall Fire two Gunns as

Quick after each other as possible and five Minutes after the same Ship shall Fire three Gunns, one Minute distance between each Gunn which is to be answered by the other Ship with one Gunn and begin to Jangle her Bell and Blow a Horn and the other is to answer by Beating a Drum and every three Minutes firing a Musquet until within Hail.

Within Hail — The Ship that Hails shall say what Ship is that which the other shall answer Earl Piercy, then the Ship that Hail'd first shall say Sir Andrew Hammond and the other shall reply May God preserve our Noble King.

A hailing trumpet.

Although Ontario never suffered attack from American forces, in the fall of 1780 soldiers of her crew took part in the raid on forts and farms along the Mohawk River of central New York.

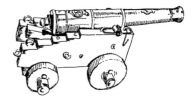

6-pounder gun.
Drawing by Rob Crothers.

Names & Captains	Rig & Guns	Year Built	Place	Year of Disposition	Remarks
Mississauga	sloop 8	1759	Oswego	?	May not have survived until the war.
Brunswick Alex Grant (1769)	schooner 6	1765	Oswego	1778 (condemned)	At Carleton Island, 6 guns?
Mercury	schooner 6	1763	Oswego	1779	"Laid up and decayed" in 1779 at Carleton, David Lyon says.
Charity	sloop or schooner	1770	Niagara	1777 (condemned)	6 swivels, destroyed at "Deer Island" (Carleton) by order of Col. Bolton, 70 tons– Charity shoal? May 1770 Edward Pollard, Sutler of Niagara Garrison, shipped goods in her.
Haldimand Burnet, Robinson Brehm, J. Andrews Laforce, Love (?)	snow 14	1770 or 1771	Oswegatchie (Osdensburg)	1782 or 1783 sank at moorings	14 guns & 12 swivels, reported in poor shape at Carleton Island 1780, "decayed," 150 tons, 76' L.O.A., 32 hands. Lying idle in 1780 for want of sails and cables, "no longer fit for lake service" and crew re-assigned, Sept. 1782 at Carleton Island.
Seneca Tushet, Baker, Bouchet, Chiquet, LaBroquerie, LaForce	snow 18	1771	Niagara	active in 1789	130 tons, 84 feet, 18 guns & 12 swivels, 45 hands. Francophone crew.. All documents and correspondence were in French.
Caldwell Baker, Fitzsimons	sloop 2	1777	Carleton Is.	1790 (made into a sheer hulk)	37 tons, 2 guns, 6 swivels, 10 hands. (Cuthbertson says 70 tons). L Col John Caldwell of the 8th came to Niagara in 1774 Mrs. Simcoe in 1793 says still in service.
Duke of Kent	schooner	1776 (?)	Carleton Is.	?	David Lyon says "built Carleton Island 1776." Perhaps bought, fate unknown. Cuthbertson says 80 tons.
Gunboat	lugger 1	1779	Carleton Is.	?	About 60' long, 36 men, 12 pounder mounted in bow, rowed.
Gunboat	lugger 1	1779	Carleton Is.	?	
Gunboat	lateen 1	1779	Carleton Is.	?	Lieut. Harrow called her "Gally".
Ontario Jas. Andrews	snow or brig 22	May 10, 1780	Carleton Is.	Nov. 1, 1780 (foundered)	231 tons, L.O.A. 95', 22 guns, 16x6 + 4x4 pdr., & 12 swivels, about 45 hands. 386 tons, says Lyon.
Limnade (Lymniad = water nymph) Baker, Bouchet, Betton	ship 16	1780-1781	Carleton Is.	c. 1793?	230 tons, L.O.A. 95', 16x6 pdr. guns. Sister of Ontario. Active in 1783, freight and Loyalist traffic; active in 1789 (see letter re: boatswain losing his arm July 23rd). At Kingston June 1793? (Simcoe)
Mohawk Chiquet	cutter 18	unknown	unknown	sold 1783	50 tons, civilian requisition (?), 18 guns, (at Oswego Oct. 1780), and searched from Niagara East Nov. 1780 for wreckage of Ontario

Armed Vessels of the Naval Department on Lake Ontario During the Revolutionary War

Sources: Geo. Cuthbertson, Freshwater; J.J. Colledge, Ships of the Royal Navy; Haldimand Papers and Letters (National Archives of Canada), Reel C 3242 RG 8 Vol 722A & others; National Maritime Museum, Greenwich London; The Lande Collection; David Lyon, The Sailing Navy List.

The October 1780 Raid

*T*he 34th company on board *Ontario* were delighted to learn in late summer that they would be included in the next raid. Their hard exercising in the whaleboats was paying off. The force would be over four-hundred men. Detachments from Carleton Island were to include at least one company from the 34th Foot, one company from the Royal Yorkers, and a few artillery-men with two light field guns, called "grasshoppers" from their strange field mounts. Fort Niagara would send two companies of the 8th Foot, three com-panies from Butler's Rangers, and a few more Royal Artillery men with another gun and a light howitzer called a coehorn. The group would be commanded by Colonel Sir John Johnson of the KRRNY, assemble at Oswego, travel in whale-boats to Lake Onondaga, then march by road to the Schoharie River and down it to Stone Arabia. The settlements of Schoharie and Stone Arabia were the fur-thest objectives. Because of the lateness of the season, return to Oswego by October 30th was ordered. The purpose of the raid was the destruction of crops designated to supply the Continental Army and to tie up rebel forces in defensive roles. A party of Iroquois volunteers under Captain Joseph Brant would act as an advance guard to ascertain the whereabouts of the enemy.

In late September, *Ontario* sailed from Carleton Island with an east wind, towing two strings of boats. Her decks were crowded with troops as well as

Royal Artillery button c. 1780.

Mohawk, Seneca, and Onondaga scouts, canoes and supplies. Her own detachment of the 34th had stowed their barrack boxes in the hold (never to see them again), and were now dressed as land soldiers. At Oswego they shook hands and exchanged jibes with their friends the sailors, all of whom had turned out in full dress to do them honour as they filed ashore. East winds were too scarce to waste, and within the hour *Ontario* was under way again bound for Niagara, passing her sisters *Seneca* and *Mohawk*, who were beating upwind, much delayed, to Oswego with the raid troops from Niagara on board. No salutes were exchanged, however. Much gunpowder had been expended firing gun salutes in the early years of the war, as whenever ships passed on the lake, courtesy called for a full salute. The captains claimed that this firing gave their crews useful exercise and a little fun. It also de-scaled the guns. In the spring Frederick Haldimand had ordered an end to salutes, perhaps fearing that a distant attack might be mistaken for harmless politeness and so be ignored.

Ontario's shortage of crew, with the marines gone, was of little concern, as the only real threat was via the Oswego River, now dominated by friendly forces. In any event, she was to pick up a detachment of another 34th battalion company at Niagara for transfer to Carleton Island.

Perhaps because of the unusually deep snow of the previous winter, the 1780 grain crop of western New York was exceptional. The importance of this bounty to the hungry Continental Army was well known to Sir John Johnson and General Haldimand. The long series of raids from Lake Ontario down the Mohawk Valley had forced General George Washington to assign a considerable garrison to the area. Johnson and his officers, after much thought, decided that a right hook from Onondaga Lake across country to the Schoharie River would bring them up behind the forces watching the principal north-south routes via the Wood Creek portage or Canada Creek. Boats would take the composite battalion up the

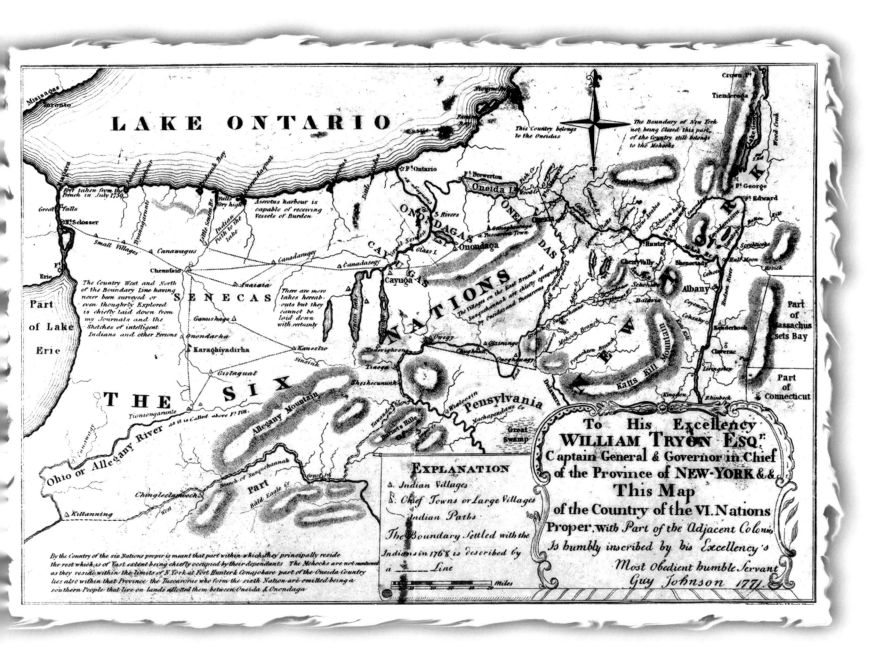

Grasshopper gun tarped for travel and with shafts in place.

Oswego River to the fork, then west on the Onondaga River, south to the head of the lake. Hiding the boats, the party would march along the Iroquois roads carrying all the supplies and ammunition on their backs until wagons and horses could be captured. Perhaps a few horses might be bought from the Onondaga for delivery at the lake. Some of these would haul on sleds or drags the four light artillery pieces (three grasshopper guns, a coehorn howitzer), their shot and shell; the others would provide mounts for the officers. In the event, all the officers' horses had to be eaten when other food ran out.

The force of about seven hundred that started out from Oswego on October 1st included two hundred and sixty-five Iroquois under three chiefs, Sayequeraghta (Old Smoke), a seventy-year old Seneca of the Turtle clan; Captain Joseph Brant of the Mohawks; and Chief Cornplanter, a young Seneca of the Wolf clan. From Niagara, Colonel John Butler brought two hundred rangers (four companies); one hundred and forty men (two companies) of the King's Regiment, 8th Foot, sent by departing Lieutenant Colonel Masson Bolton; and a ten man detachment of Royal Artillery, 4th Battalion. From Carleton Island Sir John brought one hundred and fifty of the 1st Battalion KRRNY (three companies) under Major James Gray and eighty men of the 34th Foot under Captain Andrew Parke, including *Ontario's* detachment.

Each of the troops was issued with sixty rounds of ammunition, a new blanket, fringed buckskin leggings, and a pair of moccasins. The rolled blanket was carried slung over the left shoulder; haversack (with provisions) on the back, knapsack on the left, cartridge pouch, combined bayonet and hatchet frog both on the belt. The issue tomahawk was vital for building rafts and lean-to shelters, cutting firewood, and clearing blocked roads. Occasionally it served as a close-combat weapon. Each man also carried a sheath knife, and if he chose, a tarpaulin jacket.

As mentioned before, units on the frontier had been ordered to cut the men's second tunics off short, just below the waist, for wear on bush patrol. The faded scarlet was darkened to rust-red and the coloured facings removed. Hat brims were cut off except for a peak, and a few partridge feathers added by many. White cross belts and musket slings were darkened or exchanged for tan.

The leggins were gartered with a thong just below the knee and each had a belt-loop for support. The moccasins were worn over bare feet. In cold weather a square of cloth or kerchief served as a sock, held on by a ribbon under the arch, crossed over the instep and tied around the ankle. Some soldiers could knit, so had real socks, mitts, sweaters, tuques and scarves, to their greater comfort and the envy of their comrades. Yarn was obtained by unravelling issue blankets.

No waterproof clothing or groundsheet was issued in 1780. However, the resourceful soldier as a rule equipped himself with a tarpaulin jacket, made usually aboard ship from old sail-cloth or condemned tenting, plus Stockholm tar. Without these, pneumonia would have taken more lives than enemy action.

The parade ground "Number One" uniform was left in the soldiers barrack box when a raid was on. Grey fatigue trousers and grey fatigue shirt replaced the white britches, shirt and neck stock, providing an inconspicuous target for the enemy. The Rangers were similarly dressed and equipped, but wore dark green jackets in place of rust red. The Royal Yorkers of Sir John Johnson had originally worn green, but by 1780 had switched to red with facings of blue. At the time all "Royal" regiments in the British army used blue facings .

"Fatigue" means work party in the army. The rough canvas work shirt and trousers issued to each man were called "fatigue dress," both then and until quite recently. Histories usually depict soldiers of the Revolutionary War in full dress uniform, although most of their waking hours were spent hewing logs, blasting stone, splitting shingles and doing a hundred necessary tasks, all in basic grey.

All in all, the pipe-clayed "lobsterback" of the parade ground had been,

3-pounder brass "Grasshopper" gun reproduction at Fort Henry. Note ammunition box on the trail and iron brackets for horse shafts. Diameter of bore 2.913 inches; roundshot 2.775; cannister (or case) 2.77. As a shell, it fired the land service grenade (also 2.77 inches) weighing about 2 pounds.

Colonel John Butler (1728-1796), Commanding Officer of Butler's Rangers.

Butler's Rangers belt-plate (above left), cartridge pouch monogram (middle left), and button (below left).

Sir John Johnson (1742-1830), Major-General of Militia and Colonel of KRRNY, Commander of the October raid in 1780.

Seneca War Chief "Cornplanter," the son of a Seneca mother and an Irish father. From a painting by F. Bartoli.

Captain Joseph Brant "Thayendanegea" (1742-1807), Mohawk War Chief and principal Iroquois commander. From a painting by Gilbert Stuart.

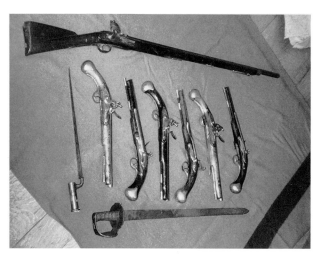

Sea-service musket, bayonet, sea-service tanged pistols, and cutlass (top).

"George III" monogram from a cartridge pouch (middle) and from a 6-pounder gun (right).

by 1780, re-designed. Training in Indian-style warfare was exhaustive for both officers and men, and it paid off in reduced casualties and more successes. After a few years of service in the 8th or 34th, the young men from Liverpool or Cumberland, in constant association with old frontiersmen from the Rangers, had learned fieldcraft, woodcraft, survival in the wild, resourcefulness, musketry, concealment, and teamwork. They could fire up to four aimed rounds a minute from their heavy (14 pound) Brown Bess flintlocks.

Musket ball and powder came in a cartridge paper tube tied at each end with pack thread. To load, the cartridge was torn with the teeth, a little priming powder poured into the open pan, the frizzen (or pan-lid) closed, the rest of the powder poured down the barrel, and the bullet and paper rammed down after it. Handling the ramrod was a time-consuming part of the drill. For speed, after firing, the musket was half-cocked, leaving the pan closed. Then all the powder was poured down the barrel, in hopes that enough would find its way out the touch-hole into the pan. Slanting the weapon a little with the pan down helped. Then the bullet was dropped in free, the wax paper discarded, and the butt banged smartly on the ground. The "bang" ensured that the bullet was firmly home and that a little powder was forced out into the pan. The musket barrel was bored .75 inches diameter and the balls were moulded fourteen to the pound or about .70 inches. This left one-twentieth of an inch space or windage — a very loose fit — resulting in loss of range and accuracy without the wadding of paper. Effective range was about 60 to 80 yards.

The bayonet was triangular, about 17 inches long, its leather scabbard carried in a frog slung from a cross-belt over the right shoulder with a hatchet added. Half a dozen spare flints and a brass pick for cleaning the vent were carried in the cartridge pouch on the front of the belt. The pouch held nine ready-use cartridges. Fifty-one more (to start) were carried in the knapsack.

BITE, POUR POWDER, BULLET, POUND, COCK and FIRE! All with the ramrod left in its sleeve! (Caution: keep the barrel up, or the bullet may roll out.) The steel ramrod was too useful in roasting rabbits and grouse to be thrown away, and besides, it was needed for cleaning.

The raid did not go as planned, though it was eventually successful. Marching in ankle-deep mud along the rain-soaked dirt roads, wagons stuck and men started to drop out. Twelve were left behind to make their own way back to the boats. The brass howitzer, heaviest of the artillery, and its shells were buried in a swamp. But despite these problems the plan succeeded. Enormous quantities of grain were destroyed — six hundred thousand bushels by one estimate — thirteen grist mills, some saw mills, and also about one thousand barns and houses were burned. Food was no longer a problem, but several sharp actions were fought with American forces. Efforts to reduce two forts were unsuccessful without the howitzer. The little three-pounder guns were useless against stout walls and time was in favour of the defenders.

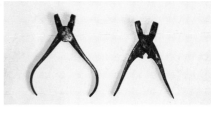

Several references in American reports are not complimentary to the Royal Artillery. Attacking the fort at Schoharie, all of their shells burst either too short or too long. None fell in the fort. The fuses probably had suffered in the long, wet march. On October 19th one of the 3-pounders was "taken" by the Americans, "complete with implements." Lieut. Driskil, an American artillery officer, carefully listed the "29 round Shott, 12 Canister, 120 lbs. corn Powder, Quadrant, Fuses, 2 Port-fires, Auger, Mallet, Punch, Powder-measure, Weigh-bar, 4 pound Weight, 1/2 pound Weight" captured. No shells are mentioned, which indicates that they had all been fired at Schoharie. This gun may have been abandoned.

Brass powder flask for priming gun locks. Musket with frizzen (pan lid) open. Bullet moulds for casting pistol balls.

British casualties were only nine killed, two wounded, and fifty-two missing. Many of the missing were simply lost and eventually turned up at Carleton Island. Others were taken prisoner. The report of only "two wounded" is remarkable. East of the fort on Carleton Island is an extensive graveyard and

6-pounder gun lock.

among the many musket balls recovered at the island are several deformed ones bearing the marks of human teeth. With no anaesthetic, army surgeons amputated wounded limbs while the patient was strapped down, biting on a bullet to ease his agony. Other raiding parties must have brought home large numbers of wounded. Over one hundred Americans were killed, including Colonel Brown, their commander at Stone Arabia.

On October 24th Johnson's group reached the boats on the return journey. They set out for Oswego on the 25th. Going with the wind and the river's current they arrived the next day. Butler's Rangers, the 8th Foot detachment, the artillerymen, and most of the Iroquois rowed on to Niagara, after a couple of day's rest in the ruins of Fort Ontario at the Oswego River mouth.

The company of the 34th looked in vain for the brig *Ontario*, their floating home, expected to be at the Oswego rendezvous "the end of October," as ordered by Sir John. They would never see her again, and with her went several wives and children of the regiment. All of their kit, save what they wore, was lost. *Seneca* took the Carleton Island half of the party home downwind, towing the whaleboats.

Ontario Founders

After sailing from Oswego to Niagara in early October, *Ontario* made a routine trip down to Carleton with a load of pelts and a few passengers, then returned again to Niagara late in October before preparing to pick up the raiding forces at Oswego on October 31st.

Captain James Andrews, although enjoying the comfort of the new and larger vessel, was glad to spend a few days ashore at Navy Hall with his wife and daughters. His friend Lieutenant-Colonel Masson Bolton had commanded the 8th Foot "King's Regiment" for several years, and lately was also commandant of Fort Niagara, across the river from Navy Hall. Colonel Bolton was in very poor health, his teeth decaying and poisoning his entire system. Like many of his men, he had suffered from scurvy the last two winters when supplies ran short. The principal anti-scorbutic prescribed by the battalion surgeon was spruce beer, a remedy only partly effective. Winter rations of apples and vegetables had been used to save starving Iroquois refugees, thousands of whom had flocked to the fort after their farms had been burned, fruit trees chopped down and cattle driven off by a strong rebel force in 1779.

This humanitarian act had hit Bolton very hard and he had asked Haldimand to grant him leave to visit a dentist in England. His replacement, Brigadier H. Watson Powell, had just then come up in *Ontario* to relieve him, a bitter pill since command of the garrison and the upper posts should now merit brigadier rank, just when he departed.

View of Fort Niagara with Navy Hall in the foreground. From a painting by James Peachey.

Fort Niagara from the American shore, 1784.
From a painting by James Peachey.

Sir John Johnson had ordered that "the large vessels be off Oswego at the end of October to cover embarkation, in case of pursuit by the American forces." At Niagara, *Ontario* boarded a thirty-seven man detachment of the 34th Regiment for passage to garrison duty at Carleton Island, plus some P.O.W.'s, four Indians, one civilian merchant, an artillery warrant officer, and several other soldiers. Colonel Bolton was assigned half of Captain Andrews' comfortable quarters in the stern. The four women and five children, dependants of the 34th men, took the berth area in the hold.

A farewell parade and lunch for Colonel Bolton occupied the morning of October 31st. Mindful of his orders, Captain Andrews was anxious to sail as soon as possible, and cast off about 1:00 p.m. to the "bon voyage" cheers of the paraded 8th Regiment for their commanding officer.

By late afternoon *Ontario* was off Golden Hill, about 30 miles east of Niagara, running before a fresh south-west wind. Brigadier Powell, who reported this sighting, failed to say by whom, but it was to be the last. In the same letter to General Haldimand he said that "about 8:30 in the evening a sudden violent storm struck from the north east."

Next morning, November 1st, a party of Rangers returning to Niagara from Oswego along the south shore of the lake, came upon the boats from *Ontario*, washed up, along with blankets, oars, her binnacle, gratings, part of one of her quarter-galleries, and Commodore Andrews' hat. Later, other hats, some clothing, a sand-glass, and a compass were also found. Powell had the schooner *Mohawk* and foot parties search 55 miles of shoreline (he does not say where the starting point was) without finding anything else. Neither wreckage nor spars were found, although a further search by bateau was carried out the following August under Lieutenant Crowe. Perhaps this was done after six bodies came to the surface about 12 miles east of Fort Niagara in the last week of July 1781.

The Great Hurricane of October 1780, the most devastating in one hundred years, had arisen 3,000 miles away in the Caribbean. On October 10th it sank a Royal Navy vessel the size of *Ontario* off the island of St. Lucia, the HMS *Beaver's Prize*, formerly *Oliver Cromwell*, 248 tons, a privateer captured from the Americans. She mounted sixteen 6-pounder guns. She was not alone. The same day HMS *Cornwall* (74 guns) and HMS *Vengeance* (32) sank nearby, while at St. Vincent HMS *Experiment* (50) was lost.

Martinique was struck October 12th. Forty French ships went down, including the new French frigate *Juno* (40) taking with her over three hundred crewmen. Also three British frigates, HMS *Andromeda* (28), HMS *Laurel* (28), and HMS *Deal Castle* (24), sank. The West Indies Squadron lost HMS *Thunderer* (74), HMS *Stirling Castle* (64), HMS *Phoenix* (44), *LaBlanche* (42), HMS *Scarborough* (20), HMS *Barbadoes* (14), HMS *Camelon* (14), and HMS *Victor* (10). Few of their people survived. It was a very black month for the Royal Navy. As well, over one hundred merchant ships foundered or were driven ashore at great cost to Lloyd's of London, the insurers.

The hurricane continued northward, striking Bermuda on October 18th and taking toll of a further fifty ships. Veering a little to the west, it crossed the New England coast, then struck Lake Ontario a few days later. The north-east wind mentioned by Brigadier Powell would be the westerly part of the counter-clockwise hurricane, probably with winds upwards of 80 knots, which, after dark, would strike with little warning.

In late October, Andrews would be using his heaviest canvas. Being late for his appointment at Oswego, he may not have taken the usual night-time precaution of reducing sail. By holding to 6 or 7 knots he could reach Oswego in about 20 hours from Niagara and pick up his share of the raiding party for Carleton Island. Contemporary drawings by James Peachey and others indicate that no "Royals" were carried by lake vessels. However, Peachey shows very deep topsails, so that even double-reefed, a considerable area of sail was

A *compass card, 1780.*

PART OF LAKE ONTARIO

PLAN
OF
NIAGARA
EXPLANATION

RIVER FROM LAKE ERIE

NAVY HALL

provided by fore and main courses plus topsails. Her cross-jack (cro'jack) was really a main-yard so that down-wind her 'trysail' (called 'spanker' in later times) was brailed up to the gaff and mast and a large square main course set, rendering her a pure square-rigger before the wind.

Running comfortably toward Oswego in the cool fall evening, she would have one watch on deck, everyone else settled for the night. There would be disappointment when the south-westerly wind died away rather suddenly, though perhaps for experienced sailors, a measure of concern. When out of the north-east a line squall of appalling force suddenly struck, probably accompanied by sheets of freezing rain or a dense wet blizzard, shouted orders could not possibly be heard over the screaming of the wind in the rigging and the thunder of slatting sails. The very newness and strength of her sails and rigging would work against her. Instead of blowing to ribbons and reducing the wind resistance, they held firm, pressed against the masts. The gale striking over the port bow from the north-east would back all sails, slewing her head to starboard, throwing the helmsman away from the tiller. Broadside on, she would careen to the starboard ends of her beams, her spars and sails dipping the cold seas, until the masts snapped or were pulled right out of their steps and overboard. (The diver who discovered the wreck reports only empty holes, no mast stumps; however, stumps might have floated free long after the sinking.)

The sudden knock-down would create havoc below decks. Her main armament was sixteen 6-pounder guns, eight per side, on wooden carriages, including two on the foredeck as bow-chasers. She also carried six 4-pounders on the quarter-deck. All guns were secured by tackles when under way, but turn the ship 90 degrees onto her side and all hell breaks loose. The starboard guns on the low lee side lunge forward, smashing their muzzles into the gun ports, snapping their fastenings and forcing all closed ports open, with the guns jammed in the two foot high openings. All this is underwater now. The gun deck is flooded knee deep in minutes, water pouring over the hatch coaming into the hold.

All the ready-use 6-pounder cannon balls would have fallen out of their garlands between the guns and crashed straight down, 24 feet across the now-vertical deck. The galley stove, sea-chests, furniture, and her sleeping people would be hurled down to the lee side. Those on the platforms in the hold would fare no better. The ballast of useless old cannon, shingle, and granite field stones is packed along the keelson, but only the guns are fastened down, in order to get at the bilges for flushing dirt (otherwise bilges tend to reek.) Some of the ballast, cargo, and reserve ammunition would roll right down to the deck beams.

Furthermore, the portside guns would be hanging suspended by their tackles from eye-bolts never intended to stand such strain. One of these may well have broken loose and dropped down onto the struggling people in the flooding starboard side. Another gun may have crashed around in the commodore's cabin aft, knocking loose one of the quarter-galleries (the bay-windows on each side of the stern). This gallery washed ashore to be found the next morning.

On deck, the first onslaught would send the watch tumbling, but someone must have cut the lashings on the boats. Blankets may have been brought up to protect the fortunate few who might have made it to them. On the other hand, the blankets may have been kept in the boats, just in case, or they belonged to people who were sleeping on deck.

Somehow both masts went overboard, probably allowing the vessel to partially right herself, despite the pressure of the wind, although listing badly because of the ballast and cargo shift. The emergency response to this situation must have been to run out the high-side guns and possibly to force some of the low-side guns out the gun ports and into the lake. We know that seven guns

A *sketch of* Ontario *caught in the storm.*
By Peter Rindlisbacher.

are scattered on the slanting upper deck. These are probably the two bow-chasers and five quarterdeck 4-pounders. Circumstances at the time would have prevented even the bravest men from venturing on deck to jettison anything. The hull, including the main deck, is full of silt, so it remains to be seen whether the crew managed to lighten *Ontario* by dumping some 6-pounders out the gun ports.

The diver who discovered the wreck reports that the visible guns are all "cocked up" with quoins removed. Guns were normally fully elevated when secured against the possibility of bad weather. Down in the gun-deck the muzzles would be lashed to a ring-bolt over the gun port and the run-out tackles drawn tight. On the upper deck they were hauled to the centre line and lashed in pairs with muzzles crossed. The vessel is slightly more stable with guns here, and there are more ring-bolts available to tie them down.

Commodore Andrews' hat indicates that he was on deck at the time of the initial assault, but no orders could be heard over the wind and probably none were given. It would be impossible to hear anyone, even below.

The four boats carried by *Ontario* were likely built to Admiralty standard, as they had to stand up to hoisting in and out frequently. They were probably even painted to keep them from drying out in the sun and to look a little smarter. One of the smaller boats would usually be towed astern for convenience, in good weather. It is even possible that in preparation for loading men at Oswego all of them were in tow, as Oswego harbour had no deep-water wharf. At the time, a vessel clearing for action put all boats overboard to reduce the danger of flying splinters and also to avoid their destruction or perforation by shot and musket ball. Colonel Johnson had warned the Captain to expect American pursuit, so this may be how the boats came to break loose and wash ashore at Golden Hill where the raiding party returning from Oswego found them. The painters simply snapped, releasing the boats to drift away.

When the raiding force had reached Oswego, they split up and went their separate ways. Some headed to Carleton Island on board *Seneca*. The remainder, men of the 8th foot, Butler's Rangers, and Iroquois scouts headed for Niagara in their boats and canoes. For tired rowers it is a long pull of several days duration. The south-west wind was no help, although the lee of the south shore of the lake meant calm water. At dusk, they made for shore to make camp for the night.

By 8:00 p.m. on October 31st, most of the older men had turned in, sleeping under the boat's sails for extra warmth. The rest were sitting around the fire on driftwood logs laughing and talking. A few likely had blankets over their shoulders to ward off the late autumn chill. Their muskets were stacked nearby, the primed locks wrapped in rags to protect against the dew.

Suddenly all fell silent, as from the distant north-east a noise like that of a host of ducks taking off came to them across the quiet lake. A dash to haul the boats up clear of the beach followed. A short while later a wall of rain and spray, driven by the shrieking wind, struck the camp. Away flew the sails, the blankets, and even the firewood. Trees went down along the edge of the bush unnoticed. The men huddled in the lee of the boats, unable even to speak above the roar for several hours. By dawn, the wind had died away. Fires were started to cook breakfast and dry out.

There remained 40 miles or so of hard rowing before reaching Fort Niagara, and an early start might just make it possible in one day. A few miles along the way, however, the party was again ashore. Four battered boats had been discovered, along with oars, blankets, and clothing, washed up over a half-mile stretch. A binnacle and part of a quarter-gallery indicated that a large vessel had come to grief during the storm.

A frantic search for survivors in the bush brought no result. No bodies were found. A Ranger lieutenant found a naval officer's three-cornered cap, the turned-up brim edged in gold braid. Inside was a label reading "J Locke; hat maker: St. James: London." The initials "JA" for James Andrews were

Naval officer's hat.
From a painting by Dominic Serres.

punched in the pigskin sweatband, confirming that the wreck must be the new brig *Ontario.*

Two Mohawks, both strong paddlers, set off by canoe with a despatch, taking the Commodore's hat. A cairn was erected to mark the area for future searches.

When he heard the Ranger's news, Brigadier General H. Watson Powell, the new Commandant at Niagara, wrote to Governor Haldimand. Parts of his several letters follow, together with one from Captain Fraser at Carleton Island:

To: His Excellency,
General Haldimand

Niagara, November 10th, 1780

Sir/

*   * * * * * We are under great Apprehensions for the Ontario, which sailed from hence on the 31st October with Colonel Bolton, Lieut. Royce and 25 of the 34th Regiment. A violent Gale came on that evening about eight o'clock, and from several of her Gratings, Oars, part of her Quarter Gallery, Binnacle and other things being found upon the Beach the next day by the Troops returning from Oswego, there is no doubt that she must have suffered considerable damage, even if she is not lost. I have since sent the Mohawk to ask along the Shore, but nothing more has been found, she must therefore have foundered, if she has not been heard of at Carleton Island, of which the Commanding Officer there will of course have informed you as he was informed of the time she sailed from hence.*

*   Should Your Excellency have received Confirmation of this terrible Event & of Colonel Boltons' being lost in the Ontario; as the King's Regiment is now under my Command, I think it incumbent on me to recommend them in the strongest Manner to Your Protection, and as they have upon some occasions,*

when Vacancies have happened in the Army, been considered as not belonging to the Line. I hope they will now be looked upon in the same Light, and that the Promotion will go in the Regiment. * * * * * { I send a Duplicate of the return which Colonel Bolton carried with him.}

I have the Honor to be, Sir,

H. Watson Powell

Brig'r Gen'l., Command'g at Niagara

Carleton Island 8th November, 1780

Sir,

I am exceedingly sorry to inform your Excellency that the New Vessel (the Ontario) is in all probability lost, and every person on board of her has perished; Amongst the rest Colonel Bolton, Lieut. Royce with the Detachment of the 34th which was at Niagara, Lieut. Colleton of the Royal Artillery, and several other Passengers, together with Capt. Andrews and all the Officers and Crew of the Vessel.

She sailed on the 1st Ins't in the afternoon. A most violent Storm came on the same evening from the Northeast, wherein she is supposed to have overset or foundered near a place called Golden Hill, about thirty miles from Niagara, as her Boats, the Gratings of her Hatchway, the Binnacle, Compasses, and Glasses & several Hats, Caps & different wearing apparel & Blankets were picked up along shore by Col. Butler on his way from Oswego to Niagara. This account is brought by the Mohawk which is just arrived from above after having searched all the south side of The Lake without having made any other discovery of the Ontario.

I have thought necessary to dispatch a Boat to Canada immediately to bring Your Excellency, as early tidings as possible of this Misfortune, as it must affect the Arrangements in this Quarter.

Capt. Andrews is an irrepairable loss to the Department he belonged to.

Capt. Bouchet of the Seneca who says he had Col. Boltons leave to go to Quebec (as he is ready to set off) will have the honor to deliver this letter.

I have the honor to be with great respect.

 Sir, Your Excellency's,

  Most obed't and Most humble Servant

   Alex'r Fraser

   Commandant, Fort Haldimand

To: His Excellency,
General Haldimand

         Niagara, November 18th, 1780

Sir/ The Seneca which left Carleton Island on the 13th instant brings a letter from Captain Fraser acquainting me that no account has been receive'd there of the Ontario, which, I am sorry to say, confirms her Loss, in the opinion of Everybody, beyond a doubt; a blow which must be long severely felt by this communication, particularly in regard to Captain Andrews, an Officer of much Approv'd Worth, that I am afraid Your Excellency will find it very difficult to meet with a person in every respect qualified to succeed him. The consequences of a divided Command have already, I am informed, been attended with circumstances detrimental to the Service, which could not be so well known to anybody, as to the Officer Commanding the Troops at Carleton Island, where Captain LaForce commanded on shore and Captain Andrews on the Lake; the consequence was that difficulties frequently arose about things demanded from the Naval Store, or about loading the Vessels, which must have been prejudicial to the Service, had not Captain Andrews been possessed of that happy coolness which induced him to prefer the Public good to his Private feelings. As it may be difficult to find a Person, who will always have sufficient Command of himself to know when to enforce his Authority, or when to give up particular points, I hope Your Excellency will appoint somebody to succeed Captain Andrews, whose Command in that Department will be supreme both upon the Shore and on the Lake, which will prevent Disputes that may sometime prove fatal to the Service. I am also informed, that the instant the loss of the Ontario was known at Carleton Island, violent disputes arose between the Captains LaForce & Bouchette about the Command, which perhaps would not have been easily settled, had not the former have gone down to Canada. Captain Bouchette had likewise permission to go there, & had given up the Command of the Seneca to Lieutenant Choquet, but upon the loss of Captain Andrews he re-assumed the Command & has since been very active in forwarding the Service. Captain Andrews always carried his Papers on board with him, when he went from hence, & it is probable some may have been lost with him, which his Successor may stand in need of. I am sorry it is necessary to mention there is great want of Naval Stores, not only upon this communication but upon Lake Erie. The Haldimand has been lying idle all this Summer, for want of Sails & Cables, and the Sails of the Seneca, Captain Bouchette informs me, are in so bad a state, that it would be risking too much to venture her another trip this stormy season, which might not only have reduced the Garrison to some difficulties in regard to Provisions, but must certainly very much affect the Commercial People, as it will now be impossible to transport much of their Merchandise. The Upper Lake is likewise in a want of Cables.

I transmit a Return of the People lost in the Ontario & likewise a copy of a Paper which Colonel Bolton carried with him, containing the Surgeon's opinion of the cause of the sickness which prevailed at this place.

Knowing Your Excellency's attention to the families of the faithful Servants of the Crown, I beg leave to represent to you that Captain Andrews has left a Widow & three Children here, and as his Circumstances, I am told are not very good, they will become entirely dependent upon his Brother, if you do not grant them some assistance. And now I am on the subject of asking favors; the King's Regiment recalls my Attention to them & I hope you will pardon me, if I once more recommend them to your Protection.

Captain Fraser has sent me the copy of a Letter which I fancy you have by this time received, containing the Master Builder's opinion relative to the building of two Schooners; I shall send every possible assistance from hence that no time may be lost in putting your commands in Execution so soon as they shall be known.

I have desired Colonel Johnson to send some Indians to Winter at Carleton Island. He promises as many shall go, as can be prevailed upon, but says he is afraid there will not be many, as they are cautious of returning on board a Vessel since the loss of the Ontario.

I have the Honor to be with great Respect, Sir, Your Excellency's most humble Servant,

    H. Watson Powell A.L.S.
    Brig'r Gen'l., Command'g at Niagara

To: His Excellency,
General Haldimand

                                        Niagara, December 4th, 1780

Sir/

* * * * * A Party returned two days ago, which have been fifty five miles along the Shore to see if they could discover any remains of the Ontario, but nothing was found, except the few things which were before reported.

I have the Honor to be with great respect, Sir, Your Excellency's most obedient & most Humble Servant,

                                        H. Watson Powell A.L.S.
                                        Brig'r Gen'l., Command'g at Niagara

A·L·S·

Brigadier General Powell's signature.

Brigadier General Powell reported that the following people were on board *Ontario* and "must be presumed drowned":

CAPTAIN JAMES ANDREWS, *The Naval Department,*
    Commodore of the Lake Ontario vessels
LIEUTENANT-COLONEL MASSON BOLTON, *King's Regiment (8th Foot),*
Commandant of Fort Niagara
LIEUTENANT PLAU, *The Naval Department*
LIEUTENANT CHARLES S. COLLETON, *Royal Artillery*
CONDUCTOR TIG [OR PIG], *Royal Artillery (Warrant Officer)*
LIEUTENANT SOUTHWELL ROYCE, *34th Regiment Detachment Commander*
2 sergeants, 1 corporal, 1 drummer, 30 privates *(34th Foot)*
4 women and 5 children *(wives and family of the 34th men)*
2 privates of the *8th Regiment*
2 rangers *(Butlers)*
1 gunner private
1 passenger *(civilian)*
4 Indians
29 seamen [or 40 as stated by Haldimand]

No prisoners-of-war are listed by Powell. Names were reported only for the officers and warrant officers killed and missing in those times. The 34th Regiment detachment served as marines, but on this voyage they were also passengers in transit. Red coats are seen on all of Lieutenant Peachey's watercolours of Provincial Marine vessels. The two Artillerymen may have been part of the crew as well.

Rations were provided for women or wives accompanying infantry units on a scale of seven per company of seventy men. Obviously children were also tolerated. It would be thought wiser that the women and children remain in port, but the contribution of the wives to food preparation and laundry on

Silhouette of Captain James Andrews.

board must have prevailed. The group may have been in transit to Carleton Island, so were not typical. This is borne out by Governor Haldimand.

He says in a despatch to London that the men of the 34th on board were crossing the lake to re-inforce Carleton Island. He also mentions the loss of forty seamen in this letter. To man twenty-two guns plus twelve swivels and sail the ship would require close to one hundred men, so, if this detachment of the 34th was put ashore at Carleton, others would be required to take their place, probably part of Captain Andrew Parke's company, returned from the raid.

When it became certain that *Ontario* had foundered, these men of the 34th wrote to Haldimand asking for compensation for the loss of "all their kit except what they wore on the raid" in *Ontario*. Soldiers are always practical. Several officers wrote to seek promotion in the 8th Regiment, particularly to command. The other naval captains vied for Captain Andrews' job, with some bitterness. One of those disappointed quit the lake, for a time.

Elizabeth Andrews wrote a sad letter requesting a pension. It appears that Mrs. Andrews did receive financial assistance and was able to stay on in the Niagara vicinity. Probably James' brother Collin, a merchant at Detroit, helped her. William Canniff, writing in 1869, states that her daughters both married army officers, and that their descendants are named Sheehan, Hill, and Givins. The son returned to Scotland.

The Toronto Reference Library has some letters found in Mrs. Andrews' effects after her death. Two of these, written by Captain Andrews to Collin in 1779, probably were given to Elizabeth by her brother-in-law as keepsakes. Letters to her are addressed to Newark, then, in 1792, to Detroit, c/o Thos. Forsythe Co., then in 1822 to York. Collin had epilepsy, returned to Ayreshire and died destitute in 1791. He even sold his furniture to buy food for his sons near the end, the letters tell us. The Andrews' granddaughter, Miss Maude A. A. Givins, was in possession of a silhouette portrait of Captain Andrews.

This is now in the John Ross Robertson collection.

Efforts to suppress news of the tragedy failed. In late November eight Oneida prisoners were released at Fort Niagara, and on December 9th their leader, Jacob Reed, an interpreter, gave a full account to the American commandant at Fort Schuyler. William L. Stone, writing in 1838 in his "Life of Joseph Brant" says: "The prisoners taken from Stone Arabia, after reaching Niagara had been shipped for Buck Island, in the river St. Lawrence, but from the long absence of the vessel, and the fragments of a wreck, drums, furniture etc. which had been washed ashore, it was believed she had been lost and that all on board had perished."

34th Regiment Drum.

The actual examination of Reed was written and sent to General George Clinton, Governor of New York. It is preserved:

Q 21:   *What Vessels are at Niagara?*
A: *One 16 gun Frigate and three small Sloops.*
Q 22:   *What is become of the Prisoners lately taken at Stone Arabia,*
         Tryon County?
A: *They were sent away with Captain Powers to Buck's Island, and it is*
         said are Cast Away, as Drums, hen Coops, Tables etc. are daily Cast
         on Shore on the Lake.

(The eddy current near the mouth of the Niagara carries flotsam to the South shore over a great distance from the river.)

Watson Powell said nothing about any P.O.W's in his report to Haldimand, but James Andrews mentioned taking prisoners down the lake in a 1779 letter, so apparently it was the practice. The loss of these unfortunate soldiers would not affect any unit strengths, and no replacements would be required; hence it was not essential to include them in the casualty return. Protocol, however, would dictate that General Haldimand notify the Americans of the deaths once he knew of them. Doing so would disclose the drastic change in British fire-power on Lake Ontario caused by the loss of *Ontario*.

So Powell had his reasons for silence, if in fact Jacob Reed knew the truth. No account of prisoners taken at Stone Arabia is given by Stone, but he says that General Van Rensselaer, the American commander in the North, had learned from a prisoner where Colonel Johnson had hidden his boats. Sixty men under Captain Joshua Vrooman were sent to destroy them. Instead, the Americans were ambushed. Four were killed and the rest, three officers, eight NCO's and forty-five privates, captured. As this happened on October 23rd, it is likely that these prisoners would be in Niagara a week later, sent on ahead with the wounded. Captain Vrooman is not heard of again.

Twenty of the prisoners (probably all privates), claimed to be serving under duress, swore an oath of allegiance and joined the KRRNY. This left thirty-six POW's in the group.

Jacob Reed's story indicates that the loss of life in *Ontario* was considerably higher than first reported. Can he be believed? He mentions "drums and furniture." This conflicts with the list given to General Powell by Colonel Butler. Perhaps the drums and furniture were picked up by junior ranks and converted to beer money at Niagara. No point in turning them over to authority. As a prisoner, Jacob Reed would hear these details on the grapevine, and would also know about other prisoners taken from the P.O.W. enclosure for transfer to Buck (or Carleton) Island. The important intelligence was that a 22-gun Canadian vessel had foundered. He would gain no reward for bringing bad news about Americans well known to his examiner at Fort Schuyler (née Fort Stanwyx, now Rome, New York), so he is believable.

Francis Goring, who lived at Niagara in 1780 and was well acquainted with all details of the disaster, puts the number lost at "about 120 Souls" in a letter to his uncle. Consequently about thirty prisoners were on board if the seamen mustered twenty-nine, and if the correct number of sailors was forty, as Haldimand later reported, then about nineteen Americans were drowned. This tragic shipwreck constitutes the worst loss of life ever suffered on Lake Ontario. The terrible *Noronic* fire was, of course, at a slip in Toronto harbour, not on the lake proper; one hundred and nineteen people died in that disaster.

*W*as *Ontario* a bit top-heavy? Of her main armament, fourteen 6-pounders were on the lower deck, about as close to the waterline as was prudent. The 6-pounder weighs 16 hundredweight for the 6 foot length and increases with half a dozen various lengths. The 9 foot long model weighs 24 hundredweight. Hundredweight (or cwt) is a British measure equal to 4 quarters (qtr.) or 112 pounds (lbs.). All guns had their weight in cwt., qtr., and lbs. engraved on the breech ring by the foundry. Many brigs of her size were armed with 9-pounders or even 12-pounders — much heavier guns. In the season of fall gales, normally a captain might stow a few of his guns securely in the hold to lower the centre of gravity. Anticipating a pursuit by the Rebel forces, Andrews could not do this.

The twelve swivel guns weighed about 100 pounds each. They were carried in the hold until needed, but anticipating a dawn battle with the Americans, the captain would have them all on deck, mounted in their sockets. In addition, the six 4-pounders, at 6 hundredweight apiece, were most likely all on the quarterdeck, and two chasers, at a ton each, on the fo'c'sle.

To accommodate a greater bulk of cargo, *Ontario* was designed with a rounded hull. Brigs designed for speed in despatch work appear to be more vee-shaped and hence more stable, as well as faster. The Royal Navy, however, had a large number of brigs quite similar to *Ontario* and must have been satisfied with their design. Even so, *Seneca's* experience when she had to sacrifice six brass guns does cast doubt.

In 1778 the brig *Seneca* had nearly been lost in a storm off the Main Ducks Islands. She was saved by dumping overboard six of her guns. Unfortunately these were all brass, and much more valuable than iron guns. Orders came out that henceforth no brass guns would be used aboard lake vessels. A court of enquiry exonerated her captain, and the lesson was learned. Brigs were dangerous on the lake, although in January of 1779 *Seneca* still carried eight 9-pounder guns and ten 6-pounders. As she was 84 feet long on deck, had a 73 foot keel, and 24 foot beam, she was almost the same size as *Ontario*. Captain Schank had noted that he intended "putting into her six pounders only, and reducing the number of gunns to fourteen."

The Brig-Sloop of two masts had become a separate class in the Royal Navy of 1780. By 1786 there were fifteen on the list carrying from fourteen to eighteen 6-pounders. By 1805 the class numbered sixty-four, obviously a popular model.

The Admiralty draught clearly shows *Ontario* as a brig of two masts. Surprisingly, the divers report three apparent mast holes in the wreck. Captain Andrews must have elected to opt for the third mast and rigged as a "snow" or "senault," as the French accounts spell it. This would explain the rig of *Limnade*, her sister ship, built at Carleton Island the next year using the draught and patterns of *Ontario*. This is not the 1800s model "Snow" with a snow-mast set very close to the mainmast, but following the style of the mid-eighteenth century, with the short mizzen mast stepped midway between the mainmast and the taffrail. Maritime historian G.A. Cuthbertson says "Snows were vessels of three masts square-rigged on the fore and main masts and lateen rigged on the mizzen." The fore part of the lateen sail was abandoned, and the rest hooped to the mast as a "driver." It was loose-footed. The Admiralty draught does not show any signs of an optional mizzen mast, stepped on the lower deck beams, although this was not uncommon practice in the Revolutionary War period. And indeed, it must be admitted, several prominent authorities vote for a "snow mast" or "trysail mast" close to the main mast of *Ontario*, rather than a mizzen with lateen yard as described for the lake snows of 1756, such as *Halifax*.

In a letter dated November 20th, 1780, Haldimand refers to "the loss of the new Snow *Ontario* of 16 guns." He also refers to her later as a "ship pierced for 14 guns." These remarks indicate not only possible departure from the rig laid down by the Admiralty, but a reduction in armament. The two bow gun-ports may have been only for optional use in a chase, and seven 6-pounders a side made up the main battery, plus the six 4-pounders. We may know the answers soon; they lie under the deep silt on the lake bottom.

A major inconsistency appears in the correspondence having to do with the loss of *Ontario*, namely the disparity between Governor Haldimand's and Brigadier Powell's reports concerning the number of seamen drowned. Haldimand states forty in his letter to Germain, no doubt based upon the latest nominal roll in his desk. (Several pay-lists from the Lake Ontario vessels have survived, but unfortunately not one for *Ontario*). Powell reports twenty-nine seamen lost. What happened to the "missing" eleven crewmen? Fortunately, there are a few clues suggesting a possible explanation.

Other letters having to do with the October raid written by Colonel Bolton to Sir John Johnson state that many of the garrison at Niagara were seriously ill. Bolton doubted his ability to provide the full number of men requested for the October raid. This would apply equally to infantry of the 8th Foot and to the Royal Artillery. Indeed, only about ten gunners were despatched from Fort Niagara to the Oswego assembly point. The October 1780 raiding force took along three guns and one howitzer. Each of these called for a six-man detachment, plus drivers for horses, signallers perhaps, and an ammunition party. At least thirty men in total would be needed, and this does not allow for many casualties. So the artillery troop needed to find qualified people somewhere outside its own ranks.

Besides being a cargo carrier, *Ontario* was a floating artillery battery. Her twenty-two heavy guns each required a crew of highly trained gunners to produce rapid, accurate fire against an enemy. Gun drill was almost a daily feature of life aboard ship, although a limited supply of gunpowder and round shot restricted the frequency of live firing. However, in the short time after the river froze each winter and before the crew dispersed to other seasonal employment, target practice was carried out at Carleton Island. The vessels were moored in such a fashion as to provide overlapping fields of fire for defence against a possible American attack across the frozen river. Wooden targets, usually old worn-out bateaux, were set out on the ice at varying distances. Further back, a long snowbank was built to arrest the spent balls for re-use. (A small reward encouraged the garrison in the search for these.) The guns of Fort Haldimand, high on the bluff, also participated in the target shooting, with a modest degree of rivalry between the seamen of the vessels and the Royal Artillery on the ramparts and in the blockhouse on the point. The crew of *Ontario*, drafted largely from *Seneca* and *Haldimand*, were well trained in the handling of naval artillery and won as many bets as they lost. All were good candidates to join the raiding party.

Sir John Johnson calculated that his force would require four bateaux to transport the artillery and about thirty whaleboats to carry the infantry. Some coxswains for the boats were already chosen, mostly old rivermen from Butler's Rangers and the KRRNY, but ten or so seamen would be a valuable addition to the coxswain list. The journey up the Oswego and Onondaga Rivers was fraught with danger because of the many rapids along the way. Eleven boat-canny seamen from *Ontario* could make an important contribution to the successful ascent of the rivers.

A balance would need to be struck between a useful well-trained shore party and a manageable but short-handed *Ontario*. Lieutenant-Colonel Guy Johnson, brother of the force commander Colonel Sir John Johnson and

A 12-pounder on the fort ramparts.
From a Microcosm by William H. Pyne.

Superintendent of the Indian Department at Niagara, suggested selecting those sailors who had some previous experience as engagés in the river bateaux, on the grounds that reaching Lake Onondaga by boat was the first difficulty to be overcome. He lent one of his white officers, Lieutenant Maguire, to coach the seamen in Indian ways, fitting them with moccasins and leggins, plus artillery accoutrements, and to teach them some geography of the Mohawk Valley. On the raid, poor Maguire was shot through the thigh at the Stone Arabia battle. He crawled into the bush to escape capture, but it was many days before his loyal Senecas came back to find him, by then close to death. Their Iroquois remedies saved his life as well as his leg.

If, in fact, the artillery party was topped up with the eleven *Ontario* volunteer seaman-gunners, then the stratagem was not completely effective. The American author, Colonel Stone, though writing somewhat after the event, had the benefit of many eye-witness accounts of the raid and his own boyhood conversations with relatives living at Stone Arabia. Of course these were very partisan recollections, but the details of the British artillery fiasco at Fort Schoharie could not have been invented. Blame *Ontario's* sailors.

Afloat, all seamen were armed with pistol and cutlass, which they handled skilfully, but they would not be as familiar with the flintlock muskets now issued to them, and although well trained in 6-pounder drill, they had no experience with the grasshopper field piece. Nor would they have much experience with fixed ammunition (the powder charge is in a flannel bag attached to the base of each projectile), for the navy in 1780 used only separate 'ammo'.

Worst of all, the vessels' guns did not fire shells, so the men would know little about time fuses and the cutting of them to proper length for air-burst over the target. Naval ammunition then included round shot, grape-shot, case (or canister), bar-shot, and chain-shot, but at the time no fused hollow shell. Paper cartridges were used for gunpowder charges on board ship, but field artillery used attached flannel charge bags. That very year, 1780, Captain

Schank refused his approval of fixed ammunition for use on the lake vessels.

This inexperience in fusing shells is perhaps what caused the artillery problems at Fort Schoharie. The first shells fired at Schoharie sailed right over the fort, sputtering in their flight and landing somewhere out of sight. For ensuing shots, the propellant charge was reduced and the fuse length cut. These rounds burst far short, to the derisive cheers of the American garrison. The unfamiliar task of adjusting the charge, the fuse, and the elevation of the guns to achieve a burst on or over the target was perhaps too much for the volunteer seamen.

Naval gunnery proved to be a different matter entirely from the precision required of field artillery in order to be effective against a fortress. The guns did, however, do a good job at Stone Arabia in the open field. Against American infantry and cavalry the case shot inflicted many casualties. Each canister contained about three dozen large iron pellets weighing over an ounce apiece. At short range these spread out in a very lethal cone. No fuses to go wrong. Four rounds per minute were fired by each grasshopper, while the enemy remained within range. The American commander was killed, as were many of his men, mostly by the artillery fire.

However difficult these eleven seamen may have found their duty as artillerymen, they were spared the fate of their shipmates on board *Ontario*, though it may have occurred to the experienced sailors that, had her full complement been aboard, *Ontario* would have more swiftly struck her topgallant masts, closed her deadlights and buttoned up for heavy weather. More muscle available to heave guns overboard and to man the pumps just might have saved their vessel from foundering.

Ontario's Sistership

*L*est the change in fire-power on Lake Ontario encourage a counter-raid or invasion by the Americans, repairs were started on the old *Haldimand*. She had been lying idle at Carleton Island most of the summer, not quite condemned, but short of sails and cables.

The "*General*" *Haldimand*, Captain Love, is listed by Lloyds on January 7th, 1781 as having sunk in the St. Lawrence River with the loss of one man drowned. She probably sank at her moorings in North Cove that November 1780. The General mentions this loss to Lord George Germaine, Colonial Secretary, in a letter of November 20th, 1780.

Lord George Germain
by a Guernsey Vessell
Lieut. Caldwell

Quebec 20th Novr. 1780

My Lord,

I take the opportunity of a Schooner bound to Guernsey to do myself the Honor of acquainting Your Lordship that the Fleet which last Sailed for this place is not yet arrived — **** It is with great Concern I acquaint your Lordship of a most unfortunate Event *which is just reported to me to have happened upon Lake Ontario, about the 1st Inst. a very fine Snow, carrying 16 Guns, which was built last Winter, sailed the 31st Ultimo from Niagara, and was Seen Several times the same day near the North Shore — The next day it blew very hard, and the vessels boats, Binicle, gratings, some Hats, etc. were found upon the opposite Shore, the wind having Changed Suddenly, by Lieut. Colonel Butler about 40 miles from Niagara on his way from Oswego. So there cannot be a doubt that She is totally lost and her Crew consisting of 40 Seamen perished, together with Lieut.Col.'l Bolton of the King's Reg't whom I have permitted to leave Niagara on account of his bad State of Health/ Lieut. Colleton of the Royal Artillery, Lieut. Royce and 30 Men of the 34th Reg't who were crossing the Lake to reinforce Carleton Island: — Capt'n Andrews who Commanded the Vessel and the Naval armament upon that Lake, was a Zealous; active & intelligent officer. The loss of so many good Officers and Men is much aggravated by the consequences that will follow this misfortune in the disappointment of conveying Provisions across the Lake for the Garrison of Niagara and Detroit which are not near compleated for the Winter Consumption and there is not a possibility of affording them much assistance with the vessels that remain, it being dangerous to navigate the Lake later than the 20th Inst., particularly as the large Vessels are almost worn out, the Master Builder, and Carpenters are Sent off to repair this Evil. *****

I am sorry to acquaint Yr. Ldship that three of the Homeward Bound Fleet, one of them (the Haldimand) a rich Furr ship, are with their cargoes totally lost going down the River — the Crews are safe.

I have the Honor to be etc.etc.

(signed) Fred. Haldimand

Perhaps there were two *Haldimands*, but this is unlikely. Any vessel with that title would be Canadian-built, one would think, or at least Canadian-owned. The "Cargoe of Rich Furrs totally lost" may have been insured at Lloyds.

Nominal rolls of crew on Lake Ontario use the full title *General Haldimand*. She must have been successfully raised as she served through the summer seasons of 1781 and 1782. On September 13th, 1782 Captain Ancrum reported that "the snow *Haldimand* is no longer fit for lake service, and her crew is put into two gunboats."

Her bottom and lower rib sections sit today on the west side of Schank Harbour in about 10 feet of water, held firmly in place by a quantity of rock which appears to have been dumped down the hatch after she sank. No doubt this was done to prevent her moving, and to convert her into a permanent wharf.

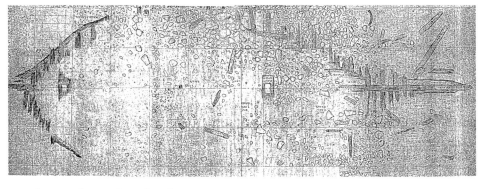

Remains of Haldimand in Schank Harbour (North Cove). The two mast steps are prominent. Note all the rocks dumped in to hold her in place.

Work was rushed on the second brig, *Limnade*, on the stocks in the island shipyard. Contemporary drawings show *Limnade* as ship-rigged. Perhaps her first captain wished to spread his sail area over three masts instead of two and over a larger number of smaller sails.

By Christmas of 1780 it was evident that all of the artificers should be employed on construction of the new sister-ship of *Ontario*. Because the pine patterns for frames and knees were already made, and the construction gang was familiar with the design, *Limnade* went ahead swiftly and smoothly. John Coleman was glad to have an opportunity to employ the lessons learned in building *Ontario* and to add some refinements. Unfortunately, none of *Ontario's* crew except the 34th Regiment company was available to advise him of any design short-comings. She was launched on September 27, 1781.

In the matter of armament, it must have been considered prudent to dispense with the six 4-pounder guns. *Limnade* is listed as carrying only the sixteen 6-pounders. This would leave more room on the quarterdeck and lower the centre of gravity.

The choice of rig is traditionally up to the first captain of a new vessel, and

Limnade *(the only ship-rig on Lake Ontario at the time)* at Cataraqui in August *1783*. From a painting by James Peachey.

Commodore Bouchette elected to add a mizzen. Correspondence and documents of the time refer to *Limnade* as a ship. Peachey's drawing of Cataraqui in August 1783 shows what can only be *Limnade* at Forsyth's wharf. His detail of her masts and spars is very clear and it appears that she is landing Loyalist settlers, whom she had brought up river from Oswegatchie. She is ship-rigged for sure.

The threatened attack on Montreal via Oswego never materialized. Apparently the presence of armed vessels on Lake Ontario was a decisive factor in the Continental Army's planning for the Northern front. General Washington remembered the success of Amherst's expedition down the river, but his only move was against Oswego in February of 1783. The failure of this winter raid cost many Rebel casualties from frostbite. Sadly, the peace was already signed in distant Europe, but word had not reached the frontier.

While Cataraqui became an important port-of-call in 1783, Carleton Island continued to be the trans-shipment point for goods and passengers heading to points west. Similarly the peltries shipped to Montreal were transferred to bateaux at Carleton for several more years until the merchants had established new forwarding warehouses at Cataraqui. They knew that the new boundary line between Canada and the United States was the main channel of the St. Lawrence, but it was hard to accept the British gift of six strong garrison points to their former enemy, especially since all six (Oswegatchie, Carleton Island, Fort Ontario at Oswego, Fort Niagara, Detroit, and Michilmackinac) had been securely held throughout the entire war by Loyalist and British troops.

When John Graves Simcoe, the new governor, arrived at Kingston (as Cataraqui was re-named by the Loyalists) in 1792, the move was pretty well complete. A few men were left at Carleton as caretakers. Several guns considered unserviceable lay on half-rotten carriages. Two hulks sat in the mud of Schank Harbour, *Haldimand* against the west bank and a smaller one, perhaps *Charity* or *Brunswick*, nearby. The 1878 plan of the Fort Haldimand ruins shows both. *Haldimand's* bottom is still clearly visible, from above to a snorkeller.

Limnade made many stops at Carleton between 1781 and 1790 as shipping

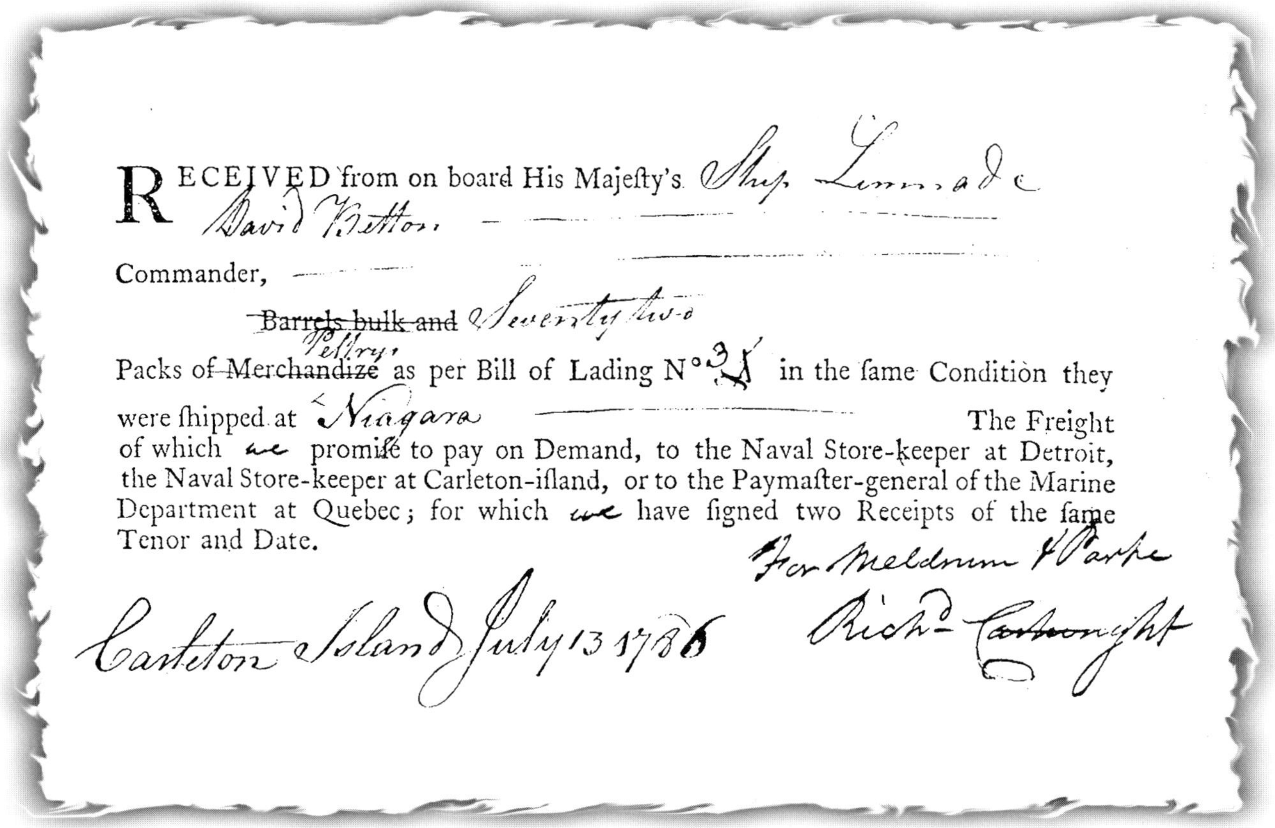

RECEIVED from on board His Majesty's *Ship Limnade*
David Betton.

Commander, ——————————————————————

~~Barrels bulk and~~ *Seventy two*
Peltry:
Packs of ~~Merchandize~~ as per Bill of Lading N° *3* in the same Condition they
were shipped at *Niagara* —————————————————— The Freight
of which *we* promise to pay on Demand, to the Naval Store-keeper at Detroit,
the Naval Store-keeper at Carleton-island, or to the Paymaster-general of the Marine
Department at Quebec; for which *we* have signed two Receipts of the same
Tenor and Date.

For Meldrum & Parke

Carleton Island July 13 1786

Rich? Cartwright

receipts show. The merchants had been prohibited from operating private decked vessels on the lakes by Governor Guy Carleton in 1777 because their numbers included several suspected American sympathisers. Forced to ship all their goods in the government schooners and snows, they retaliated by withholding payment and counter-claiming damages for delay. The signed receipts wound up as court exhibits and were preserved. One from *Limnade* is signed by Richard Cartwright at Carleton Island in 1785. Captain Betton had taken over command by then, apparently.

In 1789 *Limnade* took part in the day of rejoicing called to celebrate King George's return to mental good health. A letter from Captain Bunbury details the tragic outcome of the activities and indicates that "Lemonade" was perhaps a nick-name most often used for her:

Kingston, 27th July, 1789

Your Excellency:

It is great concern I have the Honor of acquainting you that James Bennett, Boatswain of His Majesty's Ship Lemnade unfortunately lost his Right Arm by a gun hanging fire in the Evening of 23rd Instant at the time of re-joicing took place here and at Carleton Island in consequence of the King's happy recovery, and I am still more distressed by adding to the above melancholy information of a similar accident that happended on the same Evening to George Barnhard of the Royal Artillery at Carleton Island, of wich he died before any Chirurgical assistance could possibly be given from this post.

Joseph Bunbury
Capt. 5th Regt.

Time was running out on *Limnade* when Simcoe arrived. Her tenth birthday was

1791. In a letter from York in June 1793, Simcoe refers to "the large vessel at Kingston; either re-build her or destroy her." This was probably *Limnade*, and the letter was no doubt her death sentence. Newer, smaller schooners were able to handle the shipping now that the garrisons were drastically reduced and civilian goods were transported in new private bottoms. There is no further record of her, so she probably was stripped to a hulk and towed into the mud of the inner harbour to settle.

Flying over Kingston, sixty years ago, a dozen sunken hulls could be seen clearly on a calm day. The top timbers of a few stuck up above the ice in winter, but anything that would burn had been chopped up long ago. Possibly the bones of *Limnade* are there with a few regimental buttons of the Revolutionary War to identify her. Butler's Rangers were disbanded after the war and offered land grants. Sir John Johnson's men of the KRRNY took up land around "Johnstown" below Prescott, and in Frederickburg Township on the Bay of Quinte, west of Kingston. Sir John himself obtained a large block of land and built a house in Kingston at what is now the corner of Brock and Montreal Street. Johnson Street bears his name. The 84th Royal Highland Emigrants were disbanded in 1784. Most went home but some settled not too far from Carleton Island. The presence of buttons identifying any of these three regiments would indicate a pre-1784 vessel.

Limnade's first captain, Commodore Jean Baptist Bouchette, continued in the service. He and his wife Angelique Duhamel raised a family at Fort Frederick dockyard, where he had quarters. In association with his old rival Captain LaForce, he was superintending ship construction there in 1790. He died in 1804 aged sixty-eight. The burial ground for the Provincial Marine is under what is now the RMC tennis courts, and no doubt he and other "Limnades" are there.

Afterword

*I*n August 1995 a small news item in the *Syracuse Herald* announced that the wreck of a Revolutionary War vessel, lost in 1780, had been found by Mr. Roderick Hedley, diver Mr. Richard Acer, and Mr. Larry Bowman, residents of Olcott, New York. Olcott is a small harbour about 15 miles east of Niagara on the south shore of Lake Ontario. Mr. Acer, an accomplished diver, had made six descents on the wreck. He reported seven guns visible, red with rust, scattered on the deck. The low side is buried in deep silt, very light, and easily disturbed by even the kick of a flipper, clouding the dark water to zero visibility. Nonetheless, he determined that the wreck was about 80 feet in length, lying on an angle, no masts in place. The visible wood he reported to be in good condition. Not much of the hull is above the silt, so it was a matter of both luck and skill to spot the outline of the wreck on the sonar.

The conjectural plan of the upper deck shows two 6-pounders in the bow and six 4-pounders on the quarterdeck. Mr. Acer also reported a pile of stones on the deck as well as the seven guns cocked-up, as they would be for securing when under way. The stones represent the missing eighth gun. They are ballast used to sink a pontoon. Once the targetted gun was chained to the pontoon, the net holding the rocks was cut loose and up floated the 4-pounder, carriage and all. The looting cannot be laid at anyone's door, and the gun has of course disappeared.

For thousands of years the Niagara River has worn its way through the soft

Cortland Standard, Wed., Aug. 2, 1995—9

Divers Claim They Have Found British Warship Downed in 1780

OLCOTT (AP)—Three men believe they have located an 18th century British warship that set sail along the lower Niagara River before disappearing in a storm.

The HMS Ontario, a new 80-foot ship that carried 28 guns and 89 passengers when it left for Oswego on Oct 31, 1780, was unable to withstand treacherous conditions and sank in Lake Ontario.

Olcott marine operator Roderick Hedley, diver Richard Acer and Larry Bowman believe they found the ship on the floor of the lake. They refused to discuss the location of their findings.

"Other people have been looking for the Ontario," Hedley said. "If we have found it, we have a time capsule, a relic from the past, and a potential tourist and business attraction."

Col. William Bolton, the outgoing commander of Fort Niagara, was among 89 people aboard the ship when it disappeared. Seventy-nine sailors and soldiers, four women and four Indians also went down with the boat.

If the ship is the Ontario, the British government would likely be interested because remains of soldiers and sailors could still be aboard.

Acer has made at least a half-dozen dives and claimed wood and cannons on the 215-year-old structure are in good condition.

Hedley said locating the ship is the equivalent to finding a tossed coin in the lake. Acer and Bowman found the structure by using a device that charts underwater formations, Hedley said.

"If this is the ship we think it is, it will put Niagara County on the map," Hedley said. "I would like to see a historical museum set up around the ship."

Douglas Knight, archaeologist for Old Fort Niagara and the Niagara County Parks Department, said the structure might be the Ontario or one of several ships that sit at the bottom of Lake Ontario.

Hedley said no additional dives are planned until the New York Board of Regents approves the establishment of the HMS Ontario Historical Society. A joint dive would be made with the authorities, and pictures would be taken should the state grant approval.

THE STATE

Trio claim they found 1780 warship

OLCOTT — They believe an important part of history remains trapped inside an old British warship, buried in mud and water in Lake Ontario for 215 years.

Three men have claimed they discovered the remains of the 28-gun HMS Ontario, a ship that disappeared in treacherous weather conditions after setting sail along the lower Niagara River on October 31, 1780.

Col. William Bolton, the outgoing commander of Fort Niagara, was among 89 people aboard the 80-foot ship when it disappeared. Seventy-nine sailors and soldiers, four women and four Indians also went down with the boat.

Otcott marine operator Roderick Hedley, diver Richard Acer and Larry Bowman believe they found the boat on the floor of the lake.

Acer, who has made at least a half-dozen dives, said wood and cannons on the structure are in good condition.

— The Associated Press

limestone of the region, creating the gorge and carrying millions of tons of resulting silt to Lake Ontario. Add to this a century of erosion, slowly washing all the black leaf-mould down many streams to the lake, after the primeval forest was cleared in the nineteenth century. Littoral drift moves this mixture back and forth along the south shore, affected by storms and current. Today the wreck is partly visible, but she has likely been completely buried prior to 1993 according to Mr. Hedley, as she did not show on earlier sonar scans.

Also in August 1995, Mr. Dennis McCarthy of the St. Lawrence River Historical Foundation drew to my attention a letter written on August 1st, 1781 by Mr. Francis Goring, a merchant of Niagara, to his uncle in London. In the letter he tells of the loss of *Ontario* and mentions that "about a week ago, six of the corps [sic] was picked up about twelve miles from here and buried, and believed to be from the *Ontario*, lost in November of last year." Bodies in the depths of Lake Ontario, where the temperature hovers at 40°F year round, do not suffer gaseous decomposition with its resulting bloat and buoyancy. Therefore these six had made it somehow into shallower water, perhaps swimming or on a makeshift raft.

Niagara, August 1, 1781

Dear Uncle.

* * * * *A very malancholy misfortune happened nigh here last fall. On the 31st Oct. a New Vessel called the Ontario sailed from here in the afternoon, and about 12 O'clock at Night a violent Storm arose in which the Vessel was lost and every Soul on board Perish'd in number about 120, among which was Lt. Col. Bolton, who commanded this Post, Lt. Collerton, of Artillery, Lt. Royce of the 34th Reg't. About a week ago six of the Corps [corpses] was picked up about 12 miles from here and buried, which is all that has ever been seen. This was the finest Snow that ever sailed these Lakes and Carried upward of*

Mahogany wheel barometer made in London c. 1780 by Charles Aiano.

a thousand Barrels. We have none but Indian news here, whose barbarity will not bear repeating. * * * * 'Tis said that Genl. Haldimand is going on on expedition to join _____ and bring off Allen.

I am Dear Uncle with all Respect
Your obedient Nephew,
F. GORING

To: Mr. Jas. Crespel
No. 25 Panton Street
Haymarket, London

The final resting place, though still secret, is somewhere near the town of Wilson, New York. *Ontario* must have run or drifted about 25 miles before sinking after the storm first smote her. No wreckage or spars other than that of the original discovery was ever found, although the shoreline was searched several times.

Upon the strength of this evidence, it would appear that Captain Andrews had some warning of the storm, leading us to conjecture another course of events for that night in 1780 when *Ontario* foundered. The "Weather Glass" or Torricelli Tube, a J-shaped mercury-filled tube (fore-runner of the barometer), would, if he had one, indicate a dramatic drop in pressure, perhaps two hours before the hurricane struck. Also the screech of the high winds is sometimes audible for 10 or more miles distance from the edge. The spiralling wind roars around in a huge circle, 60 or more miles across, counterclockwise, at great speed: 70 to 100 miles per hour. The whole hurricane, however, saunters along at a mere 15 or 20 miles per hour. As the system approaches, the winds die to a calm, giving those on deck a further caution.

In preparation, the auxiliary tiller would be socketed into the rudder post in the great cabin so the helmsman could steer safely below-deck, eying the fore topsail through a companion skylight. Hatches would be securely closed, and sail reduced to the minimum needed for control, basically a storm headsail and triple-reefed fore-topsail or forecourse. Topgallant masts and spars would be lowered to the deck and secured. All crew would be ordered below decks. At the last minute the captain and the on-deck helmsman would duck down the ladderway before the roaring wind and raging seas struck the vessel. But strike her they did, and partially or completely dismasted her, as well as knocking her down on her beam ends, shifting cargo and, no doubt, even some of the ballast.

With one or both 50 foot long masts, pine-tree size in diameter, crashing down, tangled in a web of rigging, it is apparent how the lee quarter-gallery was smashed off, if not immediately, then by the captive monster dragging alongside, and crashing repeatedly into the wales. No one could live who ventured on deck to attempt cutting away the wreckage. The fact that no spars washed ashore is evidence that the vessel carried her masts with her to the end, probably pounding continually. Because the winds were from the north-east, a run for the shelter of the Niagara River was the only choice.

In the centre of a hurricane or other circular storm there is an enormous updraught of air. This is what causes the dramatic lowering of barometric pressure in the whole general area. To compensate, high altitude air, extremely cold, moves downward around the fringes. This accounts for the drop in temperature as the storm approaches, and usually creates blizzard conditions in the November gales. The great storm of November 8, 1913, about which much has been written, drove all vessels on the lower lakes into harbour, onto the beach or, in the case of thirty-eight, to the bottom. Thirty-foot high waves, blinding snow, and, for the schooners, terrible icing of all spars and superstructure

Mercury barometer from the late eighteenth century, on display at the Marine Museum of the Great Lakes.

caused the sinkings, groundings, and capsizings.

Fresh water freezes more readily than salt, of course, but on the North Atlantic ice is frequently a serious concern. Royal Navy vessels in the eighteenth century, on at least six occasions, were saved from capsizing only by deliberately dismasting themselves when driven spray turned to a huge mass of ice over all spars and rigging.

If *Ontario* had warning, and if Captain Andrews did take normal precautions, battening down, lowering spars and upper masts to the deck, then he just may have been able to weather the initial blow with masts intact. We know that everything on deck was swept away at that stage because of the boats, gratings, and other articles washed ashore near Golden Hill. But perhaps a scenario different from the one set out previously should be considered. If ice did build up on the top-hamper and upper works of the hull to a dangerous level, then the masts may have been deliberately sacrificed. No one could survive on the upper deck in gale winds and icy footing, so out would come the big cross-cut saw in the gun deck. Two men would slash through the massive pine mainmast in short order. When it let go, it would rip up a few deck planks as it swung downward tearing away chainplates and snapping stays. The carpenter would have anticipated this, preparing to patch the damage from below.

Meanwhile others, in the fo'c'sle, would be attacking the 16 inch foremast with bucksaw and axes. The ice-coated masts and rigging would crash spectacularly, but no one would be on the upper deck to witness the fall. Ice-covered shrouds and stays would criss-cross the deck in a vast tangle, binding the downed spars to the hull.

In either case, the measures taken were not enough to save her. Perhaps one or both masts lies today in the silt beside *Ontario*. If so, it will be interesting to learn whether there is evidence of saw or axe on the butt.

With the boats washed away in the first blast there was no question of

Boat rudder with pintles, anchor chain, and mast step recovered from Deadman Bay.

abandoning ship. Beaching on the rocky shore would mean quick break-up under the hammering of the hurricane seas. So they would run before the storm, listing badly to starboard (the lee side when she was knocked down), pumping with all their strength to keep ahead of the leaks. To enable the winter ship-keeper to pump the bilges from inside, one pump-handle is located on the gun deck out of the weather. The wracking of the vessel in the knock-down, the damage to the planking of a broken mast hammering her side, and the green seas sweeping over her decks and down through the broken glass of the companions all added water to her pump's burden.

Mast step with iron fish-plate reinforcing bolted through from a Deadman Bay hulk, on display at Fort Henry.

If she was making 4 or 5 knots with some sort of jury rig, perhaps a sprit sail, then her crew, or those surviving, and her passengers laboured for about six or eight hours before the end. Possibly at some point they tried to run out the port guns. This would be done to correct the list as well as to raise the damaged starboard planks and the hole where the quarter-gallery had been.

To jettison the guns, each weighing over a ton, would be almost impossible in a short-handed, plunging, rolling vessel. Many of the crew would be dead or injured as a result of the initial knock-down or the attempts to cut away the dragging top-hamper. Most would be terribly seasick on top of the other problems. However, they may have managed to haul some guns across to the high side, using the tackles. Working by lantern light on a heaving deck, this would be a herculean task.

Although the storm had largely subsided, the leaks would eventually overtake the weary pumpers and it would become apparent that the goal of reaching shelter at Niagara was beyond their endurance. One would have expected an attempt to beach. Perhaps they were surprised to sink so soon. Or a final blow by the dragging mast may have smashed loose a complete plank, just at or below the waterline, letting in an unstoppable flood. With little strength left, and no time, they would be unable to improvise rafts. Those who could swim would head for the distant shore as the deck sank beneath them. The cold November lake would give them no more mercy than it did the others, left praying in the lantern-lit cabins, as the rising water surged around them.

We know that six made it into a depth at which the water temperature rises considerably in mid-summer. A tarpaulin jacket, belted and tied tightly at the wrists and neck, provides not only buoyancy, but some protection for the upper body against cold. Something like this must have helped those six who now lie in unmarked graves near Wilson. The bones of many others are no doubt entombed in the silt-laden hulk of *Ontario* in what later became, for them, a foreign land.

Some day their remains may be interred in Canadian soil, and a suitable monument erected to record this early tragedy of the Naval Department.

1/2-pounder swivel gun found in Kingston Harbour.

Limnade *off Grande Isle*.
Sketch by Peter Rindlisbacher.

Glossary

Apron: A curved timber backing inside the lower end of the stem above the keel.

Ballast: Iron, stone, or shingle placed in the bilges to lower the centre of gravity.

Beam: The width of a vessel.

Belaying Pin: A pin to which lines are made fast.

Bilges: That part of the hull beneath the hold.

Binnacle: A windowed cabinet which protects the compass, its lantern, and the sandglass watch-timer.

Bitts: Upright posts for securing lines and cables.

Bulkhead: A vertical partition.

Bulwarks: The frame ends and planking above the upper deck.

Buttock Lines: Lines on a draft that show the longitudinal hull curves at intervals parallel to the keel.

Camber: The upward curve of a beam.

Cannister Shot: A tin filled with walnut-sized iron balls for anti-personnel use at short range.

Cant Frames: Frames that are not perpendicular to the keel at the bow and stern.

Cap Rail: The longitudinal timber over the upper ends of a vessel's frames.

Carlings: Stiffening timbers bridging between and at right angles to the deck beams.

Catheads: Beams projecting from the bow from which are suspended the anchors.

Ceiling: The internal planking.

Chainplates: Iron fastenings for attachment of shrouds to the sides of the hull.

Chock: A wedge of wood.

Clamp: (also Shelf or Deck Clamp) A thick internal strake that reinforces the sides and supports the deck beams.

Coaming: Raised frame around a hatch.

Coehorn: A small howitzer: bored 4 2/5 inches: firing a.fused shell: carried in a litter slung between 2 horses.

Companion: A deck opening or skylight.

Companionway: (ladderway)Stairs between decks.

Counter: The portion of a vessel's stern that overhangs.

Courses: The principal sails, lowest on each mast.

Deadwood: Solid timbers bolted to the top of the keel at the stern.

Deck Beam: A timber that supports a deck.

Depth of Hold: The distance between the floor timber and the top of the lower deck beams at the midship frame.

Eye Bolt: A bolt with an eye at the end.

False Keel: A timber bolted to the bottom of the keel to protect it.

Fish Plate: Plate of iron used to strengthen the joint of two major hull timbers, one on each side bolted through.

Floor Timber: The lowest timber of a frame, fastened to and across the keel.

Fo'c'sle or *Forecastle*: The space under a raised foredeck.

Frame: A complete rib transverse to the keel and composed of a floor timber and several futtocks bolted together, usually nine pieces in total.

Freeboard: The height of the upper deck above the waterline.

Futtocks: The upper sections of a frame.

Garboard Strake: The external plank next to the keel.

Grating: An open work wooden grill used over a hatch in fair weather or to provide footing at the helm.

Gudgeon: An iron bracket attached to the sternpost on several of which the rudder hangs.

Gunport: The opening through which a gun fires.

Gunwale: The uppermost wale or strake atop the bulwark.

Half Frame: A frame that does not cross the keel.

Hanging Knee: A vertical iron or wood reinforcing member between the deck beams and the frames.

Head: The foremost area of a vessel, used as a latrine.

Head Sail: Any sail suspended between the bowsprit and foremast.

Keel: The backbone of a ship, to which the stem, sternpost, and frames are bolted.

Keelson: A massive long timber, over the frames above the keel, serving to stiffen the hull.

Limber Boards: The ceiling planks next to the keelson, left unfastened to permit access to the bilges.

Limber Hole: Notches in the floor timbers and first futtocks, to provide drainage to the pump well.

Lodging Knee: A horizontal brace between the deck beams and the clamp.

Mizzen: The aftermost of the fixed sails.

Oakum: Caulking material made of old hemp rope fibres saturated with pitch.

Pin Rail: A rack for belaying pins, fastened to the bulwarks.

Pintle: An iron pin on a bracket, bolted to the rudder. Each fits into a gudgeon on the *sternpost*: upon these the rudder swings.

Port Side: The left-hand side facing forward formerly called 'Larboard'.

Quarter Deck: That part of the upper deck abaft the main mast.

Quarter-Gallery: A windowed bulge on each side of the great cabin, sometime used as the officer's toilet.

Sand Glass: An hour-glass used for timing watches or measuring speed.

Scarf: (or *Scarph*) An overlapping joint connecting two timbers.

Scupper: A drain on a vessel's deck.

Shelf Clamp: (or *Clamp*) A thick internal timber that reinforces the side of a vessel and supports the ends of the deck beams.

Shell: A hollow projectile fused to explode on or above the target.

Shot Garland: A rack for cannon balls.

Shrouds: The network of ropes that brace a mast laterally and from aft.

Skeg: A projection on the keel which protects the rudder.

Snow: A vessel with a third mast, just abaft the main mast, carrying a fore-and-aft sail either on a gaff or in mid 18th century, a lateen yard.

Sprit Sail: A sail on a yard that hangs under the bowsprit.

Stanchion: A supporting post.

Starboard Side: The right-hand side facing forward.

Stays: Ropes bracing a mast from forward.

Stem: An upright curving timber joined to the forward end of the keel.

Stern Knee: A timber that reinforces the joint between keel and sternpost.

Strake: A continuous line of planks, from stem to stern.

Sweep-ports: Holes in the sides to accommodate large oars.

Swivel Gun: An anti-personnel weapon mounted in a socket, firing buckshot.

Thick Stuff: Strakes over 4 inches thick used to reinforce the hull.

Tiller: The steering handle inset in the top of the rudder post.

Top: The platform at the upper end of each mast, e.g.'Maintop' and 'Foretop'.

Top Sail: A large sail second up from the deck.

Top-Gallant Sail: The third sail up from the deck on each mast.

Top Timbers: The upper futtocks at the top of each frame.

Transom: Timber frame across the stern of a vessel.

Treenails: Wooden dowels, usually made of black locust, used to fasten hull timbers and planking, and to laminate frames.

Tumblehome: The incurving of the tops of a vessel's sides.

Wale: A thick plank that reinforces and protects the side.

Waterway: The timber running over the ends of the deck beams and notched into them.

Weather-glass: An 18th century mercury barometer.

Windlass: A horizontal winding reel turned by levers, to raise anchors, spars, cargo, etc.

Yard: A spar suspended from a mast to extend a sail.

Illustration and Photograph Credits

CWM	Canadian War Museum	NAC	National Archives of Canada		Island artifacts
DND	Department of National Defence	NMM	National Maritime Museum, U.K.	ROM	Royal Ontario Museum: Sigmund
MWM	MacLachlan Woodworking Museum	OFH	Old Fort Henry: St. Lawrence Parks		Samuel Collection
MMGL	Marine Museum of the Great Lakes		Commission	SLRHF	St. Lawrence River Historical
MTRL	Metropolitan Toronto Reference	OFNA	Old Fort Niagara Association		Foundation
	Library	PrColl	Private Collection of Carleton	A.B.S.	A.B. Smith

6 Ontario off Fort Niagara. Peter Rindlisbacher.

8 Major General Jeffery Amherst (1717 - 1797). Courtesy of NAC.

9 The British squadron on Lake Ontario in 1756. Courtesy of MTRL.

10 Prow of Ontario I? Staff College photo. Courtesy of DND.

11 Ronald L. Way of Fort Henry (right) and C.H.J. Snider of "Schooner Days" (left) watch as the prow of what may be Ontario I is raised in 1953. Staff College photo. DND.

12 Map of Lake Ontario, Upper Saint Lawrence River, and Mohawk Valley.

15 Lieutenant John Schank, RN, (1740-1823) in later life (c. 1805). Courtesy of MTRL.

16 An Exact Chart of River St. Lawrence. Courtesy of MMGL.

17 A bateau running the Lachine Rapids, 1843. Courtesy of NAC.

18 Whaleboat. W. A. Wall. Courtesy of PrColl.

20 Sir Frederick Haldimand (1718 - 1791). Courtesy of MTRL.

21 Some of the French vessels on Lake Ontario in 1758. Courtesy of MTRL.

22 Private and Officer of the 47th Regiment of Foot,

c. 1778, parade-ground dress. Courtesy of MTRL.

22 Button of 47th Foot. Courtesy of PrColl.

23 A Soldier's Life: haircuts (upper) and laundry (lower).W.H. Pyne 1808.

24 A view of the ruins at the fort at Cataraqui, June 1783. Courtesy of NAC.

25 Robert Hamilton, Merchant. Courtesy of MTRL.

25 A trading post c. 1780. Courtesy of NAC.

26 Plans of Fort Haldimand. J.H. Durham.

27 Sketches of Fort Haldimand 1889. J.H. Durham.

28 Officer's uniform button of King's Royal Regiment of New York. Courtesy of PrColl.

28 Mrs. Grant (née Marie Lemoyne, Baroness de Longeuil, called "Mimi Baronne") in later life. Courtesy of MTRL.

29 Officer and Private of the 34th Foot, The Cumberland Regiment, c. 1778, parade-ground dress. Courtesy of MTRL.

29 Button of 34th Foot. Courtesy of PrColl.

30 Upper left: Sloop Caldwell from an unsigned drawing. Courtesy of OFNA.

30 Upper right: Unidentified topsail schooner at Niagara c. 1780. Courtesy of OFNA.

30 Bottom: In this view of Niagara the brig flies a com-

modore' pennant, so it could be Haldimand in 1779 or Ontario in 1780. Courtesy of National Army Museum, U.K.

31 The British vessels on Lake Ontario c. 1792. Courtesy of MTRL.

32-33 A chart showing 'A General Return of His Majesty's Armed Vessels by order of His Excellency General Haldimand under the direction of Captain John Schank Lake Ontario.' Courtesy of NAC.

34 A sketch of Schank Harbour. Peter Rindlisbacher.

36 John Schank, "Admiral of the Blue," in his later years. Courtesy of MTRL.

37 Manuscript letter signed by James Andrews. Courtesy of MTRL.

38/39 Drawings from an old text on shipbuilding, showing how knees and futtocks are visualized in live trees. Old text.

40 Private and Officer of the 84th Foot, The Royal Highland Emigrants, c. 1778, in full dress. Courtesy of MTRL.

40 Button of 84th Foot. Courtesy of PrColl.

41 The White Cockade. Courtesy of Colonial Williamsburg Foundation.

42 Private of the grenadier company and Officer of the 8th

Courtesy of MTRL.

113 A *sketch of* Ontario *caught in the storm.* Peter Rindlisbacher.

115 *Naval officer's hat.* Courtesy of MTRL.

122 *Silhouette of Captain James Andrews.* Courtesy of MTRL.

123 *34th Regiment Drum.* A.B.S./S.H.

128 *A 12-pounder on the fort ramparts.* W.H. Pyne, 1808.

133 *Remains of* Haldimand *in Schank Harbour (North Cove).* Courtesy of SLRHF.

134 Limnade *(the only ship-rig on Lake Ontario at the time) at Cataraqui in August 1783.* Courtesy of NAC.

136 *Receipt for Peltries.* Courtesy of PrColl.

142 *Mahogany wheel barometer made in London c. 1780 by Charles Aiano.* Courtesy of P.A. Oxley, Harrogate, U.K.

143 *Mercury barometer from the late eighteenth century, on display at the Marine Museum of the Great Lakes.* Courtesy of MMGL. Photo by A.B.S.

144 *Boat rudder with pintles, anchor chain, and mast step recovered from Deadman Bay.* Courtesy of OFH. Photo by A.B.S.

145 *Mast step with iron fish-plate reinforcing bolted through from a Deadman Bay hulk, on display at Fort Henry.* Courtesy of OFH. Photo by A.B.S.

146 *1/2-pounder swivel gun.* Courtesy of OFH.

147 Limnade *off Grande Isle.* Peter Rindlisbacher.

COLOUR SECTION:

i. *A bateau in the first stone lock on the St. Lawrence River, 1781.* Courtesy of NAC.

ii./iii. Seneca, Ontario, *and* Haldimand *at the Carleton Island anchorage in May 1780.* Peter Rindlisbacher.

iv. *Ruins of Fort Haldimand c. 1850.* Courtesy of MTRL.

v. *Shipyard at Point Frederick, Kingston, c. 1792.* Courtesy of Massey Library, RMC.

vi. *Fort Niagara from the Canadian shore, c. 1784, with* Caldwell *portrayed left and an unidentified topsail schooner centre.* Courtesy of OFNA.

vii. *Niagara River with Navy Hall (right), c. 1792.*

Courtesy of MTRL.

viii. *Left: Naval Lieutenant. Right: Master and Commander of a brig-sloop.* Courtesy of MTRL. *Below: Sea-service flintlock pistol.* Photo by A.B.S.

ix. *Left: Private of the 78th Foot (Fraser's Highlanders). Right: Field Officer of the 84th Foot (Royal Highland Emigrants) 1778.* Courtesy of CWM.

x. *Oswego.* D. Vaughn, 1767, PrColl.

xi. *An Exact Chart of the River St. Laurence.* Courtesy of MMGL.

xii. *A view of Cataraqui from Capt. Joseph Brant's house on the Cataraqui River.* Courtesy of NAC.

xiii *A view of Cataraqui on Lake Ontario.* Courtesy of NAC.

xiv/xv Limnade *(left) and* Seneca *(right) off Wolfe Island.* Peter Rindlisbacher.

xvi *Captain John Schank, Captain James Andrews, and Colonel John Butler.* All courtesy of MTRL.

Bibliography

Abell, Sir Westcott. *The Shipwright's Trade.* London: Conway Maritime Press, 1948.

Allen, Gardner W. *A Naval History of the American Revolution.* Williamstown, n.p., 1970.

Allen, Robert S., Editor. *The Loyal Americans.* Ottawa: Canadian War Museum, 1983.

Anburey, Thomas. *Travels Through the Interior Parts of America.* Sydney Jackman, Editor. Toronto: MacMillan Company of Canada, 1963.

Archibald, E.H.H. *The Wooden Fighting Ship in the Royal Navy.* London: Blandford Press Ltd. 1968.

Bond, Major C.C.J. "The British Base at Carleton Island." *Ontario History*, 58, No. 1 (1960).

British Army List 1780 and 1781.

Brymner, Douglas. *Reports on Canadian Archives.* 1884–1890, (Haldimand Collection Summary). Ottawa: Queen's Printer, 1884–90.

Burleigh, Dr. H.C. *The Loyalist Regiments and the Settlement of Prince Edward County 1784.* Bloomfield: Museum Restoration Service, 1977.

Cain, Emily. *Ghost Ships.* Place: The Hamilton & Scourge Foundation Inc., 1983.

Chidsey, Donald Barr. *The War in the North.* New York: Crown Publishers, 1967.

Clowes, G.S. Laird. *Sailing Ships, Their History and Development.* London: His Majesty's Stationery Office, 1932.

Clowes, G.S. Laird, and True, Cecil. *The Story of Sail.* London: Eyre and Spottiswoode, 1936.

Colledge, J.J. *Ships of the Royal Navy.* Annapolis: Naval Institute Press, 1987.

Crisman, Kevin J. *The Eagle.* Annapolis: The Naval Institute Press, 1987.

Cruikshank, E.A. *Butlers Rangers.* Welland, Ontario: Tribune Printing House, 1893.

Cruikshank, E.A. *The King's Royal Regiment of New York.* Toronto: OHS 'Papers and Records' Vol. XXVII, 1931.

Cumberland, Barlow. *A Century of Sail and Steam on the Niagara River.* Toronto: Musson Book Co. Ltd., 1913.

Cuthbertson, George A. *Freshwater.* Toronto: MacMillan Co. of Canada, 1931.

Darling, Anthony D. *Red Coat and Brown Bess.* Ottawa: Museum Restoration Service, 1970.

Durant, S.W., and Peirce, H.B. *History of Jefferson County, N.Y., With Illustrations.* Philadelphia: L.H. Everts & Co., 1878.

Durham, J.H. *Carleton Island In The Revolution.* Syracuse: C.W. Bardeen, 1889.

Forester, C.S. *The Age of Fighting Sail.* Garden City, N.Y.: Doubleday & Co. Inc., 1956.

Gardiner, Robert. *The First Frigates.* London: Conway Maritime Press, 1992.

Gores, Joseph N. *Marine Salvage.* New York: Doubleday & Co., 1971.

Goring, Francis. *Letters Collection.* National Archives of Canada, Ottawa. MG 24,D4.

Graymont, Barbara. *The Iroquois in the American Revolution.* Syracuse: Syracuse University Press, 1972.

Hadfield, Joseph. *An Englishman in America 1785.* Robertson, Douglas S, editor, Toronto: The Hunter-Rose Co., 1933.

Haldimand Papers: National Archives of Canada, Ottawa (British Library).

Hastings, Hugh, et al, editors, *The Public Papers of George Clinton, First Governor of New York*, 10 vols. Albany: State of New York, 1900-1914.

Heisler, John P. *The Canals of Canada, Canadian Historic Sites No. 8.* Ottawa: Government of Canada, 1973.

Hitsman, J. MacKay. *Safeguarding Canada 1763-1871.* Toronto: University of Toronto Press, 1968.

Hough, Franklin B. *A History of Jefferson County, New York.* Albany: n.p., 1854.

Howard, Robert West. *Thundergate. The Forts of Niagara.* Englewood Cliffs, New Jersey: Prentice-Hall Inc., 1968.

Katcher, Philip. *Armies of the American Wars 1763-1815.* New York: Hastings House, 1975.

King, Cecil. *His Majesty's Ships and Their Forbears.* London: Studio Publications, 1940.

Knox, Captain John. *Captain Knox's Journal.* 3 vols. Toronto: Champlain Society, 1914.

Lavery, Brian. *The Arming and Fitting of English Ships of War 1600-1815.* London: Conway Maritime Press, 1979.

Lees, James. *The Masting and Rigging of English Ships*

of War, 1625-1860. London: Conway Maritime Press, 1979.

Lees, John. *Journal of J.L., A Quebec Merchant.* Detroit: n.p., 1911.

Lucas, Sir C.P. *The History of Canada 1763-1812.* Toronto: Oxford, 1909.

Lyon, David. *The Sailing Navy List 1688-1860.* London: Conway Maritime Press, 1993.

MacPherson, K.R. "Naval Service Vessels on the Great Lakes 1755-1870." *Ontario History,* 40, No. 3 (1963).

Millar, John F. *American Ships of the Colonial and Revolutionary Periods.* New York: Norton and Co., 1978.

Moore, Christopher. *The Loyalists.* Toronto: McClelland & Stewart Inc., 1984.

Mordal, Jaques. *Twenty-Five Centuries of Sea Warfare.* London: Abbey Library, 1973.

Pool, Bernard. *Navy Board Contracts 1660-1832.* London: Longmans, n.d.

Pound, Arthur. *Lake Ontario.* New York: Bobbs-Merrill Co., n.d.

Roberts, Kenneth. *March to Quebec.* New York: Doubleday, Doran and Co., 1938.

Rodger, N.A.M. *The Wooden World, An Anatomy of the Georgian Navy.* Glasgow: Fontana Press, 1986.

Scott, Michael. *Tom Cringles Log.* London: Sampson Lowe Marston, n.d.

Snider, C.H.J. *Tarry Breeks and Velvet Garters.* Toronto: Ryerson Press, 1958.

Sommers, Jack L., and Chartrand, René. *Military Uniforms in Canada 1665-1970.* Ottawa: National Museums of Canada, 1981.

Steele, David. *The Elements and Practice of Rigging and Seamanship.* London: Printed for David Steele, 1794.

Stevens, Paul L. *A King's Colonel at Niagara 1774-1776.* Youngstown, N.Y.: Old Fort Niagara Association, 1987.

Swigget, Howard. *War Out of Niagara.* New York: n.p., 1933.

Thomas, Earle. *Sir John Johnson: Loyalist Baronet.* Toronto: Dundurn Press, 1986.

Wallace, Frederick William. *Wooden Ships and Iron Men.* New York: George Sully and Co., n.d.

Webster, Donald Blake. *Conflict in Culture 1745-1820.* Toronto: The Royal Ontario Museum, 1984.

White, William E. *The Tin Whistle Tune Book.* Place: The Colonial Williamsburg Foundation, 1980.

Whitfield, Faye V. "Initial Settling of Niagara-on-the-Lake 1778-1784." *Ontario History,* 83, No. 1, (1991).

Wurtele, Fred C. *The King's Ship.* Ottawa: Transcript of Royal Society of Canada Address, Section II, 1898.

Index